Kona's Song

by

LOUISE SEARL

This book is for the lone wolves,

be they lupine or human.

May their songs be heard.

CONTENTS

Prologue

The sun, rising with its familiar leisurely elegance over Stony Brook, gilded the uppermost branches of the trees with its first rays. The aspens, birches, maples, willows and other trees that formed the forest flourished at the higher end of the valley. Lower down, where the landscape opened out into a grassy plain, the brook which gave the place its name became apparent. It was broad and shallow, the cool, clear water catching the early light as it chattered its way over its bed of small, rounded pebbles. Its soothing murmur mingled with the rustling of the breeze through the leaves of the trees and the dawn chorus of the birds to create a tune as tranquil as it was ancient, easing the sleeping creatures of Stony Brook into wakefulness.

Then, soaring up out of the valley, another sound ascended to join with the morning verse; the most beautiful chord in all nature's great symphony – the howling of wolves.

On the crest of one of the rolling hills which enfolded the valley, listening sorrowfully as the last echo of the pack's song faded into silence, a young wolf sat brooding, wreathed in a spiral of the new day's mist.

Kona had long been aware that he was different. He had known that somehow he did not quite fit in with the other Stony Brook wolves, but he had never understood why, until the previous evening. Until the previous evening, when he had been told a tale which, though it explained everything, had turned his whole world upside-down.

1
The Last Litter

In the beginning, Kona had not been aware that he was in any way different from his litter-mates. His brother, Baru, and his two sisters, Shimook and Jareth, noticed nothing different about him either. They had all suckled together in the loving embrace of Annik, their mother, and crawled with the same curiosity about the earthen den into which she had retreated to give birth.

In those days, apart from their mother and themselves, there was only one other creature in the cubs' world, and that was Garrin, their father. He and Annik were the alpha male and female of the Stony Brook pack – that is, the dominant pair, who mate for life and are the only members of the pack to breed. Since the male is usually the more dominant of the two, he is generally considered the leader of the pack, and Garrin had led the Stony Brook wolves now for more seasons than he cared to remember. Although, like the majority of animals, he and Annik had suffered losses in their time, they had successfully reared numerous cubs in the past, all of whom had eventually left the valley to seek their fortunes beyond the boundaries of Stony Brook. But both of them felt that this would be their last litter, for they – and their siblings, who made up the rest of the pack – were growing old.

Garrin still walked with his head and tail held proudly high, as signs of his authority, and the others acknowledged his status by holding their own heads and tails respectfully lower than his, or occasionally, as a gesture of complete submission, by rolling over on their backs before him. But all of them knew that, with none of the alpha pair's sons or daughters remaining in Stony Brook, and no new wolves joining, the pack would one day die out. Its continuation now depended on some of this, the last litter, staying in the valley.

In the cubs' first days, while they were still suckling, Annik left them only to drink. Food was provided by the other pack members regurgitating it for her after they had fed, and once the cubs were no longer so dependent on her milk, they were introduced to solids in this way. They soon grew large and independent enough to abandon the birthing den and sleep in the open, like grown wolves, but since they were not yet able to join the pack on the hunt, they would be left behind at a 'rendezvous site', with one of the adults to watch over them. When a kill was made, meat would be carried back to them in the stomachs of the returning hunters.

Wolves are by nature playful creatures, and the whole pack often played together, but even when their stomachs were full and their elders were weary, the cubs were full of seemingly boundless energy. They enjoyed tug-of-war, which they played with sticks or discarded fragments of a carcass, pulling until their plaything broke apart and then starting a new game trying to snatch the pieces from each other. They took turns at chasing each other, and clambered all over the indulgent adults, who tolerated having their ears chewed and their tails pounced upon with endless patience.

But by far their favourite game was play-fighting. They would begin by circling each other, snarling in feigned anger, each holding up his or her head and tail in the dominance display and neither prepared to submit to the other. Then, suddenly, they would launch themselves with mock ferocity at each other's throats.

Of these battles Baru was usually the victor. The most assertive of the cubs, he had a tendency to fight on and on until his opponent grew tired of the game and submitted. He was also the most adventurous of them, and longed for the day when he could leave Stony Brook and, as he put it, 'see the world.'

Jareth was her brother's opposite. She was inclined to be timid, and play-fights with her never lasted long as she would submit after only a few moments. It seemed likely that she would become the next omega wolf, the lowest-ranking member of the pack, a position currently held by Annik's brother, Ollan. She differed from her siblings in having a black coat, for though most wolves are grey, they may also be black, white, brown or combinations of these.

Shimook, who was generous and kind-hearted, usually kept close to her sister, accompanying her when she ventured away from the adult wolves and reassuring her whenever something frightened her. She often defended her against Baru when his play became too rough.

As for Kona, it was during the play-fights that he first began to realize he was different from the others. Whilst they would come to grips almost immediately and scuffle to and fro, locked together, he would avoid contact, leaping clear of his siblings' charges, dodging and darting to and fro. They would strive to close with him and pin him down, but he soon proved too nimble and would often wear them out. (As could be expected, this infuriated Baru). Nobody taught Kona to fight that way, and the adults would remark that they had never seen a wolf fight that way before, yet it came so naturally to him that he did it instinctively, without having to think about it.

There were physical differences too. His fur, which was a lighter grey than most, was thicker than that of the other wolves, and his paws, in proportion, were bigger. This meant that, when winter came, he felt the cold less than the others and was able to walk more easily over the surface of snow when it settled in deep drifts across the valley.

Yet it was not such things as these that made him different in a manner that mattered. The important distinction was not something as simple as an imaginative way of play-fighting or a few small physical differences. It was more a feeling, a sense that he was not quite the same as the others. He had a peculiarly direct gaze, and there was something behind it that could unnerve the other wolves if they studied it too carefully. It was as though he knew things that they did not – things buried somewhere within him that he was unwilling or unable to reveal.

"He's a strange cub," Garrin would comment occasionally to his mate, to which Annik would reply with calm conviction: "He's *special*."

2
The Teachings of the Pack

A wolf pack is not a random collection of individuals, but a closely-bonded family group, and thus the cubs were not just Garrin and Annik's cubs, they were the whole pack's cubs. The other two adults of the Stony Brook pack – Garrin's sister Parl, who was black, like Jareth, and Ollan, the omega wolf and brother of Annik – helped with their care and education into lupine life. Since wolves do not leave their birth pack, if they do so at all, until after their second winter, and the alpha pair have a new litter each spring, there would normally have been older siblings helping too, but sadly none of Garrin and Annik's previous litter had survived.

The cubs' first lessons were in tracking. They learned to identify the scent, tracks and droppings of every creature in the valley, which of these might make a meal for a hungry wolf and which were to be avoided. Next, how to determine the age of the trail, and how to follow it if it seemed promising. This, the finding of appropriate prey, was the beginning of learning to hunt.

Wolves are not ambush predators. Rather than creeping up on their prey and taking it by surprise, they approach in it full view and run it down by virtue of superior stamina, felling and dispatching it when it is exhausted. It was a simple enough theory, but there was much for the adults to teach, and much for the cubs to learn. Different prey species often required different strategies, and it was essential to know how to select a suitable quarry from among a herd, how to separate it from its fellows, and how to attack it once they were close enough. The large hoofed animals that are the mainstay of a wolf's diet are by no means defenceless, and if the cubs did not learn to work as a team, when to hang back and when to press their advantage, and how to avoid the prey's attempts to defend itself, they risked suffering serious injury at the hooves, horns or antlers of a would-be victim.

It was necessary too that they learned to catch small prey individually, in case the pack's hunt failed, or in case they ever found themselves alone or in an area where no large prey was available, and they were also taught which bushes bore edible berries, where they grew and in what season, should they ever be unable to find anything more substantial to eat.

Eventually, in mid-summer, they were taken to observe the pack on a hunt. Crouched in the undergrowth on the edge of the forest, under the supervision of Annik, they watched as the rest of the pack loped down the valley towards the herds of elk and white-tailed deer grazing on the plain. They had chosen to hunt the smaller deer, which, though they would provide less meat, would also make for a safer pursuit. One of the herd's sentinels spotted them almost immediately and gave the alarm, so that a score of lowered, feeding heads were raised, all together, and turned in the direction of the approaching predators.

The wolves split up, Garrin and Parl continuing towards the herd whilst Ollan branched off and trotted along parallel to it. The deer, apprehensive, tried to keep watching all three wolves at once. Then, as Garrin and Parl drew closer, their collective nerve suddenly broke. They fled. From where they lay, Annik and the cubs could feel the vibration of their fleeing hooves.

The wolves, too, began to run, Garrin and Parl driving the herd before them, Ollan keeping pace at its side. The chase continued like this for some time and Kona, glancing away for a moment, noticed a small herd of moose on the opposite bank of the brook, feeding on water-plants growing in the shallows. Kona remembered when he and the other cubs had been taught to recognize a moose's hoof-prints. He had placed both front paws in one of the prints, and there had been room to spare.

Unable to recall ever eating moose-meat, he said: "Mother, do we ever hunt *those*?"

Annik and the other three cubs followed his gaze, and Annik answered: "Yes, but they can be very dangerous. A moose can weigh ten times as much as a wolf, and a kick from one of those hooves could smash your skull. And look at the size of the antlers on the bulls – they won't be fully grown for this cycle of seasons until autumn, when they'll use them to fight over the cows, but already they could toss you into the air or crush you into the earth. It takes skill and courage to take down such a formidable quarry, and you must never attempt it without the full support of the pack." She paused and then, quoting an old wolf saying, added: "The wolf who attacks the moose alone is either very brave, very foolish, or very hungry."

Shimook, looking back at the hunt, returned everyone's attention to it by crying excitedly: "Look!"

The deer were tiring. The wolves, keeping them on the move, were steadily wearing them down, and the weaker members of the herd, which offered the best opportunity for a kill, had dropped back behind their companions. Now Ollan turned in towards them, separating the weaker animals from the rest of the herd, which went hurtling on down the valley.

Caught between the wolves, the weaker deer scattered in all directions, half mad with fear and the desire to escape. The wolves, charging into the centre of the melee, singled out an old doe which limped in one hind leg and proceeded to cut her out of the herd. Parl and Ollan closed in from either side, snapping at their victim's shoulders and flanks. The deer kicked and struggled desperately as the two sets of teeth fastened into her flesh, halting her flight, but the wolves hung on and dragged her down. Garrin had her by the throat almost before she touched the ground.

The hunt was over, but before anyone took so much as a bite of meat, an important ritual had to be attended to. The three wolves stood over the carcass and howled, a particular howl that the cubs had heard before when a kill was made. Starting low, it rose progressively higher and higher before beginning to fall once again, and ending on a low note. Annik joined in, although she had not been one of the hunters this time, and then explained to the cubs: "This howl is called the Hunt Song. It is performed after every kill, and has two functions. One is simply to celebrate the success of the hunt. The other is to thank the prey for giving its life so that ours might continue, and to send its soul on to the Otherworld, the place all of us, predator and prey alike, go to when we die."

Howling was a matter almost as significant as hunting, and one in which the cubs received extensive instruction. "When you howl," Parl told them, "you must fill your lungs to capacity so that you can fling your call far and wide. And you must always hold your head up high so that the sound carries."

"There are many different howls," Ollan continued. "The first one we're going to teach you is the Contact Song. It's the easiest howl to learn, and is used by a lone wolf in search of company, or a pack trying to locate a missing member. It says simply: 'Where are you? I am here.' Listen."

He demonstrated, uttering a single, piercing note. The cubs copied him. They did not hit quite the right pitch on their first attempt, but they practiced relentlessly, and within days had mastered the howl. They then moved on to more complex songs, like the Hunt Song, and Pack Song, a chorus usually howled once a day by the entire pack, in which each wolf reinforced its bonds to the rest, and the pack as a whole announced its ownership of a territory, warning others to stay away. In this song, every member of the pack howled in a separate key, so as to make it plain to any listeners how many of them there were. The alpha male took the lowest note, the alpha female one slightly higher, and so on down the hierarchy to the omega wolf, who howled in the highest pitch.

There were also howls for special occasions, such as the Birth Song to honour the arrival of new cubs (a series of high, happy notes that tailed off into yelps reminiscent of a newborn cub's calls), and the Death Song to mourn the passing of a loved one into the Otherworld (a howl conducted in a sombre, low-pitched tone that built steadily to a crescendo and then stopped abruptly, symbolising the sudden cessation of life). The cubs were also taught the Union Song, a duet howled by a pair pledging themselves to one another as mates. It was possible that none of the cubs would mate, and that they might never require this song, but it was important that they knew it, in case any of them became an alpha one day.

"These are the howls for which there are specific notes," Annik explained, "but often we howl just to give voice to a feeling, and these songs, known as Heart Songs, are specific only to the wolf howling, and his or her emotions."

"But how do we alter our voices when we howl to create a different meaning?" asked Kona.

It was Garrin who answered. "We cannot teach you the note to howl for joy or sadness, anger or fear," he said. "A howl must come from deep inside you, from the very core of your being, so that whatever emotion you wish to express is echoed in its tone. If you howl from your heart, the sound will shape itself, and others will understand its meaning."

For many days after such teachings, Stony Brook rang with the howls of the cubs as they called to each other across the valley, and the very sky resounded with their song when at last they joined their voices to those of the adults in their first full Pack Song, to proclaim their unity as a group and their presence in the land.

3
Lupine Lore

The cubs grew rapidly. Born in spring, they had to reach almost adult size by winter, in order to endure the rigours of the season. Now that they were able to keep up, they left the rendezvous site and accompanied their elders on the hunt, starting to put into practice all they had learned. They also joined them on their forays about their territory, getting to know their home in its entirety, and adding their own scents to the pack's marking places. Such places, located at intervals along the boundaries of a territory, are marked with the urine of each pack member, leaving an olfactory message warning other wolves of their ownership and containing information about the individuals of which the pack is composed.

In addition, now that they were of an age to understand, the adults began to teach them the ancient lore of their kind. First, and most important, was the tale of how wolves came to be. It fell to Garrin, as pack leader, to explain it to them.

"In the Dawn Time," he said, "when the Great Spirit, who created all things, first breathed life into the world, he made at first only the eaters of plants to live in it. He caused the grass and the trees and the bushes and the flowers to grow in lush profusion, and the bison, the various deer species, the bighorn sheep, the pronghorn, and all the other herbivores, feasted.

All went well for a time, but then, naturally enough, the animals started to breed. As their numbers grew, there began to be less food, and no-one had quite enough. They became thin and weak, but still the population increased, and soon there was not enough food for all of them. Then the larger beasts drove away the smaller ones and took what there was for themselves, and the smaller ones starved. But the larger ones kept on breeding. Before long there was nothing at all left to eat, and then the bigger creatures found themselves starving too.

Then all the animals implored the Great Spirit to help them. He took pity on them, and gave them an abundance of new grass and leaves, more than enough to feed them all, large and small alike. But they continued to breed. With the new feed giving them new heart, the animals reproduced more rapidly than ever, and soon there were twice as many as before, all ceaselessly grazing and browsing. Before much time had passed, not a leaf, not a blade of grass remained, and they were again starving. They returned to the Great Spirit and asked him for more food. Now the Great Spirit realized that if he simply granted their request, the same thing would happen again, and knew he must find a different solution to the problem.

He decided to create new creatures, who would feed off the plant-eaters just as they fed off the grass and the leaves, who would cull the weak and the sick, the injured and the old, keeping the populations healthy and at a manageable level for their environment. And thus there came into being the predators, among them Alpha, the First Wolf. The Great Spirit said to them: 'From now until the end of time, your kind will feed off the eaters of plants, preventing their populations from growing too much. This is a great responsibility I have given you, for without you to perform this service, they cannot survive. But remember also that your prey's death means your life, and without them to hunt, *you* cannot survive. All creatures, predator and prey, are connected – each of you needs all the others. Thus, you are all equally important, and must respect each other always.'

Alpha did as he was bid, hunting for his food from among the plant-eaters and controlling their numbers. The herbivores learned to band together into herds for protection, so that there were more eyes to spot the approach of the predator, and less chance of any one individual being targeted, and soon Alpha began to wish he had companions, too. He had no-one to talk to or play with, no-one to help him hunt and share the kills, no-one to lie down with at night. He was lonely, and as the days passed the feeling grew and grew. One day, as he sat watching a herd of white-tailed deer graze together, it became so overwhelming that he could no longer contain it inside him. He lifted his head, opened his mouth, and poured out all his loneliness in a long, low howl.

This was the very first Heart Song, and when the Great Spirit heard it he hastened to Alpha's side. 'What ails you, my son?' he asked him in concern.

'I am lonely,' Alpha replied.

'Surely you do not want to be a herd animal, like your prey?' said the Great Spirit in some surprise. 'You have no need of safety in numbers.'

'No,' said Alpha, 'I do not want to be a herd animal. As you say, the members of a herd band together only for safety – they have no real feeling for each other. I wish for the love of a mate and family.'

'My son,' said the Great Spirit, 'your kind is capable of very great love, and because of this, should I grant your request, you and those who come after you run the risk of knowing very great pain. When a member of a herd is killed, the others are not unduly troubled, thinking only that they themselves have had a lucky escape. But for you, who would care deeply for the other members of his group, the loss of one of them would mean intense grief. Be sure that you understand this before you ask me to give you what you wish.'

'I do understand,' said Alpha, after a moment's thought, 'but if grief is the price I must pay for love, then I will pay it gladly. I long for companionship with all my heart. I beg you to grant me a mate, and one day, a family.'

'Very well,' said the Great Spirit, 'so it shall be.'

And so, from part of Alpha's own soul, he created the second wolf in the world, a female, to be Alpha's mate. The two paired with great joy, and from then on were known as Alpha-he and Alpha-she, forever a part of each other. And to this day, the souls of mated pairs become one, as theirs were. Their love was legend, and together they were the First Alphas, father and mother of us all."

There were many other stories of the exploits and adventures of the First Alphas, and as time went by the cubs came to know them all. They learned, too, to honour their original ancestors, to turn to them for guidance and thank them for good fortune.

The cubs made it through the winter without serious incident, to the relief of the rest of the pack – the more so because this spring, for the first time since they had been together, there were no cubs to look forward to. Garrin and Annik had mated when the breeding season arrived in mid-winter, but as they had suspected they were now too old to have more cubs, and Annik had not become pregnant. It was sad, but they could feel both glad and proud that all their last litter had survived their first cycle of seasons.

4
Summons

The juveniles continued to fill out and hone their skills over the moons that followed, and after their second winter were essentially full-grown. Kona, by this time, had developed into a fine young wolf. He was strong and swift, his bright amber eyes sparkled with intelligence, and his thick, glossy coat, always a lighter shade than most, had become a shining silver that glittered when the light struck it as though permanently spangled with frost-crystals. He was reckoned very handsome. However, he had also begun to spend more time by himself. It was not that he did not like the other wolves' company, or that they deliberately isolated him in any way, but he often felt, somewhere in the deep recesses of his soul, that there was something missing from his life, and though he could not imagine what it might be, it made him lonely even in the presence of the pack. It was like a void in his heart that yearned to be filled, that he knew would make him whole if only he could do so. But how to fill it, or with what, he did not know.

He wished there was someone he could talk to about these feelings, someone who would understand, but the other wolves could *not* understand, however much they may have wanted to. Kona could not really blame them. How could they understand him when he could not understand himself?

It was late summer when he was told the tale which changed everything. Baru had been talking since spring about leaving the pack and seeing the world, and had made it clear that he would go as soon as he felt the time was right. Jareth, by contrast, had announced that she would stay in Stony Brook, a decision which surprised no-one but delighted her elders. Shimook and Kona had not given the question of departure much thought, but on this particular evening Kona had found himself wondering if his strange dissatisfaction might be assuaged by encountering new experiences beyond the valley.

He had wandered into the forest – alone, as so often now. It had rained during the afternoon, and he was surrounded by the steady dripping of water running in tiny rivulets from the trees, where it had gathered on the surface of the leaves and in the contours of the bark.

He had awoken that morning with a peculiar feeling that hung over him like cloud over the valley. It was as though there was something at the very edge of his consciousness that he could almost, but not quite, remember. He did not know what it meant. But he knew it meant something.

Now, lost in his thoughts, he hardly heard Garrin's howl from out on the plain, calling the pack together, and did not respond to it. The other wolves did, joining their voices to his as they assembled about him, and soon the Contact Song was directed solely at Kona. Still he ignored it, for he supposed they were going on a hunt, and was in no mood to accompany them. Presently, Baru came trotting through the trees in a distinctly irritated manner.

"What are you doing here?" he said peremptorily. "Didn't you hear us howl?"

"Yes, of course I did," Kona replied, "but I don't really feel like hunting at the moment and ..."

"We're not going hunting," Baru interrupted. "Father wants you. He says he has something to tell us, and he especially wants *you* there."

"Why me *especially*?" asked Kona uncomfortably. He had an unpleasant idea that whatever it was that had been bothering him all day had something to do with this summons.

"How should I know?" said Baru. "The sooner we get back to him, the sooner we'll find out. Come on."

He turned to go and Kona rose to follow him, feeling both guilty for not answering his father's call sooner and uneasy about answering it now. The sun was sinking behind the hills as they left the forest and made their way across the plain to where the rest of the pack was waiting by the brook, gathered around Garrin. They wagged their tails in pleased greeting as Kona and Baru joined them, and Kona said to Garrin: "I'm sorry I didn't come when you howled, Father. I thought you were going on a hunt, and I ..."

"It is of no matter," Garrin said. "You are here now, and I have summoned you because there is something you, and your brother and sisters, must know. I am aware that you, and you, Shimook, have not yet considered whether or not you will leave Stony Brook to seek out packs of your own, and that you, Jareth, have chosen to stay here. But you, Baru, want to see the world and will be leaving us soon, which is why I must speak of this now. It is something you should all hear, and will explain many things to you, Kona. The

20

elders of the pack already know it, for they remember its beginning. You do not, and it is time you knew the truth."

"The truth?" said Kona hesitantly, for Garrin's face had become so solemn, and his voice so grave, that he gave the impression he was about to say something of immense significance. "The truth about what?"

"The truth about you, young Kona. About why you are not quite the same as the rest of us. You know you are different, and now I shall tell you why."

Kona looked around at each of the other members of the pack, an apprehension he could not suppress growing within him at his father's words. The elders, for some reason, seemed sympathetic, and though Shimook, Baru and Jareth looked as bewildered as he felt, they appeared less anxious.

Annik approached and licked his face fondly, reassuring. Kona, now larger than she was, looked down at her, and, for the first time in his life, found he could take no comfort in his mother's reassurance.

5
Garrin's Tale

"Though not so old as I am now," said Garrin, "I was already old when this tale began. Annik was soon to give birth to what we both knew would be our last litter, and I, feeling my age, wished to be by myself for a while. I suppose I was afraid, knowing that here was my last chance to ensure the future of our pack. Afraid, too, of the onset of time. I thought, perhaps, that I would not see another winter through. I was going away to think such thoughts as these, and if I had not, Kona, you would not be alive today."

***

It was night when Garrin left the pack and began the climb out of Stony Brook. It had been a long day, and he knew he needed to be alone with his thoughts. The sky hung heavy above him, a great mass of clouds smothering the stars and extending drifting tendrils out across the face of the full moon. A storm was brewing and the air felt close and sultry.

At the top of one of the hills surrounding the valley, Garrin paused to look out over his beloved home. It had been good to him and his pack. It was a good place for wolves, and he hoped there would always be wolves there to enjoy it. As he sat, wondering, a drizzle began to fall, a monotonous prelude to the coming storm that smudged the horizon, blurring distances so that they seemed to dissolve before him.

He turned away and moved off across the vast plain that spread out, seemingly forever, beyond Stony Brook. No wolf knew how far the great plain stretched, or what lay at its end, for no wolf had ever been that far and returned. Out there somewhere, thought Garrin, were the sons and daughters that had left his pack, running now with packs of their own. Adults, some of them probably with cubs. Perhaps he was a grandfather.

There was a small wood not far out across the plain, and, the rising wind tugging at his coat, he made for this, trusting that it would offer some shelter when the storm broke. He had just entered it when a forked talon of lightning rent the clouds, and the drizzle became a lashing downpour. A crack of thunder followed, so loud that it

seemed to Garrin to have reverberated across the sky from the edge
of the world where the sun rose to the edge of the world where it set.

Hastening further in among the trees, Garrin set about searching for
a dry spot in which to rest and think. He had not gone far, however,
when he halted in surprise at the unmistakable scent of another wolf.
It was the scent of a female, evidently alone, and Garrin, curious,
decided to follow her trail.

He found her in a clearing near the centre of the wood, huddled in
the midst of a cluster of soaking bushes, eyes closed, still as death.
She was pathetically thin, every bone in her emaciated body showing
clearly through her bedraggled hide. She had several half-healed
wounds, and the pads of her unusually large paws were sore, as
though she had been on the run for some time.

Filled with compassion, Garrin went to her and nuzzled her, unsure
whether she was dead or alive. As he did so, her eyes fluttered open
and, as they fixed upon him, she yelped in fright and scrambled
backwards as though to escape. And now he saw something which
made her plight seem all the more pitiful. Beneath her lay five
newborn cubs, unmoving and drenched by the rain despite her
efforts to cover them.

"Don't be frightened," Garrin said, raising his voice above the noise
of the storm. "I mean you no harm."

The wolf stopped, more because she was too exhausted to retreat
further than because of what he said. Her eyes were wide with fear
as she stared at him, and he tried again, saying soothingly: "I'm not
here to hurt you. Please, don't be frightened. I can help you."

As she continued to stare at him, her body shaking, he realized she
was near death, and past any help he could give. She was going to
die here. He knew it, and she seemed to know, too.

Then, quite unexpectedly, she spoke.

"He told me to run ... for the cubs ... the pack ..." she paused, grief-
stricken, and then went on: "He was badly wounded. I never knew
whether he lived ... or died."

"Your mate?" asked Garrin gently.

"Yes," she said, appearing to try to pull herself together. "My name
is Rishala."

"I am Garrin. Can you tell me what happened?"

"We were attacked. A rival pack."

"And your mate told you to run," Garrin surmised, "to protect the cubs you were carrying?"

"Yes. I wanted ... I wanted to go back. But they chased me ... I had to keep going ..."

"Your mate would have been glad you did. It was the right thing to do. I'd have wanted my mate to do the same, in your place."

"Your mate?" said Rishala, her interest suddenly aroused. "Has she ... have you cubs?"

"We will have, soon."

"So your mate ... she has milk?"

"Yes, but I don't see ..."

"Then help my cubs," Rishala implored him. "Please ... it's too late for me ... but help my cubs. If but one of them survives ... my death will not be in vain."

Garrin swallowed hard as he turned towards the cubs, for they were surely dead. They lay inert on the sodden ground and remained motionless as, one by one and with mounting misgiving, he nuzzled them. One little female. Two males. Another female. And a third male ... he stopped, amazed, as his muzzle touched the last cub, for, incredibly, he felt a faint flicker of life. A tiny heart, defiant, was beating in the torpid form.

Hope swelled in Garrin as he lifted the cub by the scruff of the neck and placed him against his mother's cold, quivering side. She licked him once, tenderly, and nudged him towards Garrin.

"He is your cub now," she said. "Take him to your pack ... and raise him as your own. But when the time is right, tell him ... tell him what happened ..."

Her breathing was shallower now, and presently her head fell limply forward, eyes tight shut. For a moment Garrin thought she was gone, and then her eyes opened again and she raised her head with some difficulty.

"Tell him to travel ... towards the setting sun," she gasped. "Tell him to cross the mountains ... through the pass between the two Great Peaks ... to find the cold land beyond. His father's land. His heritage."

She drew a shuddering breath and Garrin, looking into her eyes, saw something within them withdrawing, pulling back from life. Both of them knew her death hovered near. With a tremendous effort, she forced herself to speak once more, uttering a name.

"Call him Kona," she murmured, scarcely audible now. "Call him Kona ..."

The words sounded hardly more than the breath leaving her body in its final sigh. They were her last. And for the first time, Garrin saw on her face an expression of peace. Her suffering was over, and she had died secure in the knowledge that her remaining cub was safe.

Garrin howled the Death Song over her and her poor litter, though his voice was all but drowned out by the fury of the storm. Then he went to the lone surviving cub, lifted him again by the scruff, and, with sadness in his step, turned sorrowfully for home.

***

"And when I returned," he finished, "Annik had given birth to three cubs, who suckled alongside Rishala's son as though he was their brother."

Night had fallen during the telling of Garrin's tale, but there was a sliver of moon and by its light Kona could make out the eyes of the rest of the pack, all trained upon him. He tried to say something, but found himself unable to speak, stunned into silence by what he had been told.

He rose, quickly, and turned away, breaking into a run as Annik called his name. He could not be near the others now. He couldn't bear it. He ran, blindly, unthinkingly, neither knowing nor caring where he went, and did not notice when the ground began to slope upwards.

He stopped, panting, on the crest of one of the hills above the valley, checked by the unending sight of the great plain which had abruptly opened out before him.

He was still there when dawn broke.

6
Kona Decides

Kona was dreaming. In his dream, he was sitting beneath the hills surrounding Stony Brook, looking out across his home. It was cold – he could see his breath steaming in the air. Then he felt the gentle caress of snowflakes falling on his coat. As he watched, more snow fell and covered everything, forming a vast drift that spanned the length and breadth of the valley. And suddenly it was no longer Stony Brook he was looking at. The hills behind him became towering mountain peaks. The hills on the other side of the valley melted away, so that the snow stretched out interminably before him, seemingly without end. He had never seen this place, yet, through some inherited memory passed down to him from the generations of wolves who had run there long before he was born, he knew it. This was his father's land, his mother's land, the land that should have been his.

With the recognition came a rush of images, so rapid that he barely had time to interpret them. He saw many wolves, some wagging their tails in friendliness, some snarling in hostility. He saw a forest which looked ordinary enough, but from which emanated a fear so terrible it was almost tangible. He saw a great river, and another forest where some huge creature, shadowy and indistinct except for its blazing eyes, watched him from between the trees. He saw a weird light that flickered and wavered, carrying with it a strange impression of heat and dread.

Somewhere far away, a wolf howled – a Heart Song of desperate misery, sad and desolate and aching with loneliness. It was some moments before he realized it was his own voice.

Kona woke. His heart was pounding, for the dream had been frighteningly vivid, and he shook himself as though to shake off its influence. Then he remembered where he was, and why.

It was just after dawn. The morning mist, not yet dispersed by the rising sun, had wrapped itself around him, and shielded the valley below from his sight. It did little, however, to deaden the howls of the pack, which pierced it much as they pierced the young wolf's heart. These were the voices he had known all his life, and never before had they sounded so alien.

He sat in the dew-damp grass, looking down at his paws. They made so much more sense to him now, those big paws of his. It was only to be expected that wolves from that cold, snowy land he had seen in his dream would have large paws to help spread their weight more evenly across the surface of deep snow. Likewise, they would require thick fur like his own to provide efficient insulation against the chill.

He remained where he was whilst the sun dissolved the mist, gazing down into the valley. He had grown up here. It was the only home he had ever known, and he could not imagine living anywhere else. But Stony Brook looked different this morning – familiar, yet somehow unwelcoming. It was not the valley that had changed, Kona knew – it was himself. Stony Brook just could not feel the same to him any more. After what Garrin had told him, nothing would ever be the same again.

He lay down, resting his muzzle on his fore-paws, his thoughts a turmoil of confusion and self-doubt. They followed the same path as his thoughts the previous night, when they had led him in circles until, worn out with indecision, he had fallen asleep. Now, he wondered again who he was, and where he belonged. He was not the wolf he had always thought. Garrin was not his father. Annik was not his mother. His brother and sisters were *not* his brother and sisters. This, he felt sure, was the cause of his mysterious feelings of isolation. He knew now what was missing from his life. Would the void in his heart be filled by meeting with his real father, if he was still alive in that distant land of which Rishala had spoken to Garrin? Was it worth a journey to find out?

"I might go all the way to this land only to find out he's dead too," thought Kona wretchedly. "Or I might die myself in trying to get there. And even supposing I got there, and found him, would it make any difference? Would I belong there any more than I do here? What would I say to him? And him to me? But then, how could I live with myself if I don't even *try* to find him? Oh, this is intolerable!"

His ears pricked forward as he caught the sound of three sets of paws approaching from downhill. Someone was coming to find him. There was no point in attempting to hide or slink away, so he lay still and waited for the wolves to reach him. Soon, Shimook, Baru and Jareth appeared on the hill-top and came towards him.

27

"Please," said Kona as they crowded around him, "just leave me alone."

"We wanted to tell you something," Shimook explained. She paused, and Kona said: "Well?"

"Well," she continued, "we've decided that if you choose to go in search of this land of ... of your mother's ... well ... we'll go with you."

Kona sat up sharply. He stared incredulously at them for a heart-beat or two and then, looking pointedly at Jareth, said: "All of you?"

Jareth replied: "Yes. All of us. You're ... you're still our brother, you know, Kona."

"And I'm leaving anyway," added Baru. "If you're leaving too, we might as well see the world together."

Kona looked round at the three wolves, each looking earnestly back at him, each willing to accompany him into the wilderness and all its unknown dangers. And in that moment, his decision was made.

7
Farewell to Stony Brook

Garrin stood by the brook, the elders of the pack gathered about him. His son and daughters had said nothing the night before on the subject of his tale, and waking that morning to find them gone (though they had joined the Pack Song from a little distance off), he had guessed they were searching for the wolf they now knew was not their brother.

"What will they say to him, do you think?" asked Annik anxiously. "Do you think they'll upset him further?"

"I don't think so," Parl answered her. "They've probably gone to try and reassure him that all this hasn't changed anything between them."

"But you know what Baru's like. He might say something – he might not even mean it ..."

"Parl's right," interrupted Ollan. "They were raised together. What difference does it make to them if Kona isn't their brother by blood?"

"And as for Baru," said Garrin, "I'm sure Shimook will make sure he doesn't say anything upsetting, even by accident."

"Oh, I suppose you're right," Annik said, not speaking to anyone in particular. "But I can't help worrying. Just imagine what he's going through ..."

"Should we call him with the Contact Song, do you think?" suggested Parl. "After all, we ought to be reassuring him ourselves."

"No," said Garrin. He did not look at her as he spoke, for his eyes were fixed on something further up the valley, near the forest. Following his gaze, the other wolves saw Kona, together with Shimook, Baru and Jareth, trotting towards them. The trot was direct, purposeful, and spoke as clearly as could words of the fact that a decision had been reached.

"You're leaving us, aren't you?" said Annik, as Kona stopped in front of her.

He said simply: "Yes."

"And we're going with him," Baru announced.

Garrin showed no surprise at this, but Annik looked at Jareth and, echoing Kona, said: "All of you?"

29

"Yes, Mother. Even me," Jareth replied.

"When will you go?" Garrin asked.

"Tonight," said Kona.

"So soon?" Annik cried. "Kona, you don't have to! You ... you're as much our son as any of our own cubs. You know that, don't you? You're as much a part of this pack as any of us."

"Thank you," said Kona softly, "for telling me that. But I have to go. I have to find out who I am, and where I belong. I have to see this land where I should have been born, and meet my real father, if he's still alive. I have to at least try. Please understand – it doesn't mean I don't appreciate all you've done for me. I wouldn't be alive now if you hadn't taken me in. But how can I stay, knowing what I know?"

Annik was silent for a moment. Then, her voice very low, she said: "You're right, of course, Kona. I'd do the same in your position. Any wolf would. It's just ... you were our last litter, you see, you four."

She stopped, and Garrin continued for her: "All our previous cubs left us, as you know, and we'd just hoped that this time at least one of you might stay. It never gets any easier, seeing your cubs leave."

"We're not cubs any more, Father," Shimook pointed out.

"No," he agreed ruefully, "no, you're not. But that doesn't make your leaving any easier, either."

Garrin shook his head, as though to cast away such thoughts, and said with authority: "We hunt. One last time, all of us together."

Dusk found Kona on the crest of the hill where he had spent the previous night. The pack had killed a moose, and after feeding he had wandered up here, to be joined at sunset by Garrin. The old wolf sat silently beside the young, gazing out over the unexplored land spread out before them. Kona too remained silent, waiting for his leader to speak. The yaps and snarls of a pair of coyotes, squabbling as they scavenged from the wolves' leavings, drifted up from the valley below.

Garrin said nothing for a long while. The moon crept over the horizon and began its march along the star-marked celestial pathways it traversed each night. At last, unable to stand the silence any longer, Kona said quietly: "I'm afraid of what I might find out there. How will I find the courage to face it?"

"You possess it already," Garrin responded.

"But I'm afraid," said Kona, puzzled.

"You're afraid, but you're still determined to go," Garrin corrected him. "Let me tell you something, Kona. Courage does not mean having no fear. It means *conquering* your fear. To do something you are afraid of in spite of being afraid – that is the bravest thing of all."

Another deep silence followed, each of them retreating once more into their own private thoughts. Eventually, Garrin spoke again.

"Once you leave us," he said, "you four will be a pack in your own right, and you will be its leader."

"Me?" said Kona, startled. "But I'm not ..."

"This is *your* journey, Kona."

"I don't think Baru will see it that way."

"Very likely he will not openly acknowledge you his leader," Garrin conceded, "but be that as it may, he will still be following your lead. That makes you responsible for him, and for Shimook and Jareth. It will be your duty to them to see that your own feelings do not interfere with the needs of the pack. There will be times when this will be difficult for you – every leader faces such times. Remember then what I told you of courage."

Kona said nothing as he considered this, and presently the two wolves detected the approach of the rest of the pack. Their ears flickered and their nostrils twitched, but neither wolf turned.

"We're ready, Father," said Shimook.

"I want to remind you of something before you go," Garrin said. "A single rain-drop is as nothing, but many rain-drops make a great storm. So it is with us. By working together, we can accomplish what one wolf alone could not. We survive by trusting and depending on each other. You will need each other out there. You will have to rely on one another as much as on yourselves. Do not forget this."

"We won't forget," said Baru. There was a note of impatience in his voice that said he was keen to be off. Garrin thought it quite likely that he, at least, would forget.

"Then ... it is time," said Annik sadly. She came close and touched her muzzle to Kona's, murmuring: "Alphas be with you ... my son."

The other wolves surrounded them, nuzzling and licking each other affectionately rather than speaking their farewells.

Kona turned back to look out over Stony Brook one last time. There below him in the valley lay everything he had ever known. He felt as though he was leaving his whole world behind. But Annik was right – it was time.

With his adoptive siblings beside him, he stepped ceremoniously away from the rest of the pack and, side by side, they began to lope down the hill towards the land beyond. The elders watched with heavy hearts as the four of them set off into the unknown – Kona, his beautiful silver coat gleaming in the moonlight; Shimook and Baru, their storm-cloud grey colouring making them fade in and out of the darkness like wraiths of mist; and Jareth, her black fur blending with the night and making her almost invisible. The last litter of the Stony Brook pack were gone.

<u>**8**</u>
'Something in the Air'

Wolves are great travellers. They can travel all day or night at that easy, tireless, loose-limbed lope so characteristic of their kind. They can go on and on at its steady, unchanging pace without any sign of fatigue, their purposeful paws and steadfast strides devouring distances with unhurried and unwavering determination.

Thus, Kona and his companions could have travelled some considerable way from their home the night they departed, had they wanted to. However, they had never needed to travel any real distance before – in Stony Brook, everything they needed had never been far away. This, coupled with the strain of being away from their pack for the first time and of moving in unfamiliar territory, meant that they were in no hurry to travel as far as they could that night.

They loped along in no particular formation, Baru slightly in the lead, with Kona off to one side and Shimook behind him, encouraging Jareth, who brought up the rear. Kona had a vague feeling that they ought to be travelling in single file, though the pack had only ever done this to make the going easier in deep snow. Wisely, he said nothing about it to the others.

After a time, Jareth said hesitantly: "Um ... I was wondering ... er ... that is, I've been thinking that ... that it might be nice to hear the morning Pack Song one last time. Before we get too far away, I mean."

Baru looked scornful and opened his mouth to speak, but Shimook glared at him and he only muttered something under his breath about 'sentimental nonsense.'

"I think that's a good idea, Jareth," said Shimook, still glaring at Baru. "What do you think, Kona?"

"Sounds good to me," Kona said. "There's no need to go particularly far tonight, anyway. If we stop soon, we'll still be close enough to hear the howl and give a response – I think *they'd* like to hear *us* one last time, too."

"Then it's settled," said Shimook, pleased. "The thing is, where shall we stop? Out here in the open?"

Jareth, who had been wearing a relieved expression, looked nervous at this comment and said hastily: "I don't like the thought of that."

"Well, why not?" Baru demanded. "We never came to any harm in the open in Stony Brook, did we?"

"We're not in Stony Brook now," said Kona reasonably. "There's no point in taking unnecessary risks. There's a wood not too far ahead – you can smell it, and hear the wind in the trees if you listen carefully. We'll stop there."

The others agreed, Baru rather grudgingly, and a little further on they could make out the dark mass of the wood rising out of the plain in front of them. It had occurred to all of them that this could well be the wood where Kona had been born, but none of them felt it pertinent to say anything to this effect.

They reached the wood shortly before midnight and, though it soon became apparent that there was nothing to alarm them there, Kona entered it with some caution. There was a strange feeling of unrest about the place, as though the trees themselves were tired but unable to sleep. It was nothing specific – no sight or sound or smell – and certainly the others seemed to notice nothing unusual, but Kona was disturbed.

Before long, Shimook, Baru and Jareth lay dozing side by side. Kona, however, could not settle. He stood, looking down on his companions and shifting his weight restlessly from paw to paw. He could not stop thinking that this was likely his birthplace. It was no wonder he felt something here that the others did not. Then, as though coming to a decision, he turned and trotted away into the wood.

Shimook, who was nearest to him, was roused by the movement and, seeing him go, nudged Baru and Jareth awake with her muzzle.

"Kona's gone off by himself," she said in a low voice.

"He's always doing that," grumbled Baru. "Is it any reason to wake us up?"

"I don't think we should leave him on his own in a strange place," said Shimook.

"She's right, Baru," said Jareth. "I wouldn't want to be left alone out here."

"He wasn't *left* alone," Baru reminded them. "He went off alone of his own accord."

"Even so, I think we should follow him," insisted Shimook. She got up and set off in the direction Kona had taken, and after a moment or two Jareth and then Baru rose and went after her.

They caught up with Kona a little while later. He had paused, and was casting about as though he had been following a trail which now eluded him.

"Kona?" said Shimook, tentative. "What is it?"

Kona started as if he had not noticed the other wolves, though he must have been able to hear and smell them coming. Then, distractedly, he said: "I ... I don't know. It's just ... just something in the air, that's all. Can't you feel it?"

"*I* can't feel anything except the need to get some sleep," Baru answered irritably.

Ignoring him, Kona set off once more towards the centre of the wood, leaving a bewildered Shimook and Jareth, and an exasperated Baru, to go after him a second time. He seemed more decisive now, as though he knew exactly where he was going. The ground thereabouts was latticed with the gnarled and twisted roots of trees which had heaved themselves clear of the soil during the fury of a storm, but Kona appeared to know just where to place his paws to avoid these obstacles. The others, following with some difficulty, remembered Garrin telling them of the storm that had raged on the night he had found Kona and brought him to the pack.

Then, very suddenly, Kona stopped. They were alongside him before they were aware he had halted and were able to check themselves. They had come into a clearing, in the middle of which there huddled a small and sorry-looking cluster of bushes. Kona was staring and staring at these, an expression of bitter realization on his face. The others had to look hard before they could make out at what he was staring.

What they had assumed was a tangle of roots and fallen branches at the base of the bushes was something quite different. There, half buried beneath a drift of dead leaves, lay the sun-bleached bones of a long-dead wolf. Tufts of skin and fur clung to the skeleton in withered patches, as though reluctant to relinquish their hold on life, and within the protective circle of its paws lay four more skeletons, identical in all but size to the first.

Shimook, Baru and Jareth drew back to a respectful distance, knowing as well as Kona did who those wolves had been. Not one of them spoke or thought of speaking, but Kona, alone now in the clearing, threw back his head and howled and howled as though his heart would break.

9
Beaver Lake

It was first light when Kona woke. He had spent the remainder of the night alone on the edge of the wood, slipping away from his companions after his macabre discovery and grateful when this time they did not try to follow him.

Now, he rose and looked back over the ground they had already covered, in the direction of Stony Brook. As he stood there, Shimook came trotting through the undergrowth, breaking in on his thoughts, Baru and Jareth behind her.

"Kona?" said Shimook, unsure whether or not he would object to their presence.

"I'm fine, Shimook," Kona replied.

At this moment, the sound of howling reached them, gyring up out of Stony Brook and spreading out across the plain towards them. It was not the Pack Song they had been expecting, but a Heart Song of sadness. The four wolves listened, picking out the pitch of each individual voice rising and falling in a lilting lament at their departure. The voices of Parl and Ollan died gradually away, leaving those of Garrin and Annik singing a doleful duet for the offspring they already missed deeply. Their tone dropped steadily, their voices sinking into one another until the howling ceased.

"Now," said Kona, "we answer them."

They left the wood a short while later, maintaining a steady pace, except for brief pauses to rest, until the air began to cool and the shadows lengthen towards dusk. Then they began to look for somewhere to spend the night, and were lucky enough to come upon another wood. Here, having not eaten during the course of the day, they split up and searched for food. It was not plentiful, the wood being even smaller than the one where they had spent the previous night, and only Shimook was successful. She shared her catch, a cottontail rabbit, with the others, but naturally such a meal did not go far amongst four.

Not long after they had once again taken up their journey the following morning, a scent was borne to them on the breeze which was immediately filtered as important from among the myriad others constantly reaching their noses. It was the scent of wolves. They guessed they were nearing the home range of another pack, and, sure enough, soon after entering a forest they came upon one of the pack's regular marking places. From the scent marks, they determined that this pack consisted of five wolves, three male and two female.

"Do you think they'll mind us crossing their territory?" asked Jareth.

"Well, I don't see why they should," said Kona. "I don't think a secure, settled pack will see a few travellers as much of a threat. It's not as though we intend to stay, is it? We're just passing through."

"But we're still trespassing," Jareth pointed out.

"Perhaps we should howl, just to let them know we're here," suggested Shimook. "Then they can come and investigate and see that we're harmless before we go right into their territory and they find us there."

"Nonsense!" declared Baru. "Let's just keep moving. They might not even realize we were here until after we've gone. And if they *do* find us, and they want trouble ... well, trouble's what they'll get!"

He bared his teeth meaningfully.

"It would be better to avoid any hostility, don't you think?" said Kona.

"Well, you just said you don't see any reason why they should be hostile," replied Baru triumphantly, "so you won't mind doing what I say, will you?"

"Oh, very well," said Kona reluctantly. He did not particularly agree with Baru, but he did not wish them to quarrel amongst themselves and, so saying, they set off into the pack's territory.

Some time around midday, they reached the shore of a small lake which had apparently been created by the strategic damming of the stream that flowed into it with a mass of carefully-placed branches. A second structure, a 'lodge' built of sticks and reinforced with mud, rose out of the water near the centre of the lake. All this, along with several neatly-felled trees and the gnawed bark on the lower part of the trunks of many still standing, told the wolves that it was home to a colony of beavers. They soon spotted a number of the large aquatic rodents swimming obliviously about their business, and, though a little dubious about hunting in another pack's territory, they were hungry and simply could not resist the opportunity to fill their stomachs.

Kona and Shimook circled around either side of the lake until they were between the beavers and the lodge, into which they would normally retreat when alarmed, before dashing into the water and driving the terrified beasts towards Baru and Jareth, who lay in wait in the reeds that lined the shallows. Too late, the first beavers saw their mistake and tried to turn back, slapping the water's surface with their big flat tails in warning as more wolves plunged towards them. Baru and Jareth made short work of two of them, whilst the rest submerged and made good their escape.

Dripping wet, the four wolves emerged from the lake and shook themselves dry. A necessarily hushed Hunt Song was performed, and they settled down to eat. No sooner had they finished, however, than they heard howling from somewhere close by. It was Pack Song, comprising the voices of five wolves, and it carried an ominous undertone, full of anger.

"They know we're here," said Jareth fearfully. "Shall we make a run for it?"

"I don't think we'd get out of their territory before they caught us up," Kona replied. "We don't know how far it is to the border of their land, and even if it was within reach, they know the ground and we don't. No, we'd best just stay here and try to explain ourselves when they find us."

"What do you mean, explain ourselves?" said Baru. "We haven't done anything wrong."

"We trespassed on their territory, and we stole their food," said Jareth, looking guiltily at the remains of the beavers they had eaten.

"What are a couple of beavers?" Baru said scornfully.

"That depends on how abundant food is here," said Shimook, "and on how friendly – or how unfriendly – this pack is."

Presently, they detected the pack coming towards them from downwind, and soon afterwards they came trotting through the trees. There were no cubs among them – presumably none of their most recent litter had survived – and their leader, a brown male with a broad black area across his back, had a bitter, belligerent look about him.

"My name is Matsu," he stated bluntly. "I am the leader of the Beaver Lake pack. Which of you is leader?"

Shimook and Jareth looked expectantly at Kona, who looked back at them in surprise – and remembered Garrin's words before they left Stony Brook. Then, from the corner of one eye, he noticed Baru's indignant expression and said hastily: "The thing is, we've only recently left our birth pack, and ..."

"Is that so?" interrupted Matsu. "I see. Well, there's no room for you here, understand? And I don't appreciate wolves trespassing on my pack's territory and eating my pack's food without so much as announcing themselves."

"We ... we're sorry," said Jareth, trying unsuccessfully to keep the nervousness out of her voice, "but we didn't intend to stay, you see. We ... we were just passing through."

"And it didn't occur to you to inform the pack whose territory you were *just passing through*?" growled Matsu, glowering at her. Jareth cowered behind Shimook, who answered him: "We didn't think you'd mind, since ... well, since we didn't mean any harm."

"Oh, but we do mind, don't we?" Matsu said, glancing at the others, who glared malevolently at the intruders. "So you'd better get going before we decide to teach you some manners."

"Now just a moment!" cried Baru, who until now had been mercifully silent throughout this exchange. "Who in Alpha-he's name do you think you are, threatening us?"

"Who do I think I am? I think I'm the owner of this territory you're trespassing all over!" roared Matsu. "And now you're going to learn your mistake, you insolent litter of cubs!"

Without further orders, the pack surged forward towards the Stony Brook wolves and Kona, who happened to be in front of him, found himself suddenly charged by a snarling Matsu. His body reacted before his mind had time to think about it, leaping instinctively to one side with reflexes trained from a thousand play-fights as a cub. Matsu, expecting to come to grips, was carried past by his own momentum, and Kona was able to look round for the others.

Baru had come forward to meet the pack without the slightest hesitation and had closed with one of the males, whilst the other, somewhat deterred by his ferocity, hung back and waited for a chance to rush in and help his companion. Shimook was locked in combat with one of the females and Jareth, whimpering with fright all the while, was grappling with the other.

Matsu recovered himself and faced Kona once more. Again he charged him, and again Kona side-stepped. Matsu was rapidly becoming enraged at his inability to get his teeth into the nimble young wolf, and Kona realized he could use this to his advantage and perhaps end the battle. He waited for Matsu's next impulsive charge. When it came, he again dodged, but then, as Matsu went hurtling past, he whirled round in one fluid motion and slammed his chest, his full weight behind it, into the pack leader's side. Already off balance, Matsu stumbled and fell, and at once Kona was on him, teeth poised a hair's breadth from his throat.

"Tell your wolves to stop," he said, quietly but firmly.

Matsu struggled, growling furiously, but Kona exerted his strength and pinned him down. Matsu ceased struggling. He knew when he was beaten.

"Stop!" he commanded, and his wolves obediently broke away from Kona's companions. As they approached, Kona called out to them: "Come no closer! It will be the worse for your leader if you do."

The pack sat down a little distance off. They could see that Kona was quite capable of injuring Matsu, perhaps severely, if they were to attack, whereas if they held back Kona would do the same, and their leader would escape unscathed – except for his wounded pride.

"Now," Kona said to Matsu, "give me your word that your pack will let us leave Beaver Lake with no further trouble, and I will let you up."

"You have my word," said Matsu rather sullenly.

Kona stepped back and allowed him to rise. They stood, Kona with his head and tail held up, Matsu with his lowered in acknowledgement of his defeat. Then, without another word, the Stony Brook wolves turned to go.

10
Grassy Hollow

They were clear of Beaver Lake territory by the middle of the following morning. They had travelled – unmolested, as promised, by the pack – until dusk, when they realized that they would be forced to spend the night there. They were out of the forest by this time, and so had no choice but to sleep in the open. Jareth, in particular, was averse to doing this, but there was nothing she could do about it save complain to the others.

They rose at dawn with no mishap having befallen them and, with the rising sun casting their shadows ahead of them, continued on their way. Once past the Beaver Lake pack's boundaries, they began to relax, though Jareth was unable to keep from dwelling on the incident.

"Kona," she said, "what would you have done if the pack had attacked you back there? When you had Matsu pinned to the ground?"

"I don't really know," Kona confessed. "I just did what seemed right at the time. I'd have had to wound him, I suppose, and hope that would stop them. And if it didn't, or if they'd waited until I let him up and then attacked us ... well, we'd just have had to run for it."

"Running away is for cowards," declared Baru.

"Sometimes discretion is the better part of valour," said Shimook. "Would you rather have stayed around to be injured?"

"And another thing, Shimook," Baru went on, ignoring her last remark, "why did you and Jareth look at Kona when Matsu asked who was leader?"

"Well, he's the one who's leading us on this journey, isn't he?" replied Shimook. "He's going to the cold land, and we're accompanying him. I'd say that makes him leader."

"It does not!" cried Baru. "A leader has to be dominant over the other wolves of his pack, and I've no intention of submitting to Kona, I can assure you!"

"I never asked you to submit to me," said Kona, feeling very uncomfortable with this turn in the conversation. "I didn't ask anyone to call me leader. If Shimook and Jareth want to, that's up to them, but no-one's saying you've got to."

Baru made an indeterminate noise in his throat and trotted off ahead of the others. Shimook came to Kona's side and, in a voice pitched for his ears alone, said to him: "I think you dealt with the situation at Beaver Lake very well, Kona. Jareth was too frightened to appreciate it, and Baru is too stubborn to thank you – or even to admit he has anything to thank you *for*. But the Beaver Lake wolves might have wounded us quite badly if you hadn't done what you did."

"It ... it's possible," said Kona awkwardly. "Thank you, Shimook."

For many days after this, they travelled over a fairly nondescript landscape, catching whatever small prey happened to cross their path, until, late one afternoon, they came upon what looked like a very shallow valley – a great dip in the grassland, surrounded by low, rounded hills. On the top of one of these hills, they found the scent marks of another wolf pack, this one composed of ten wolves – five male and five female, including two cubs.

"After what happened at Beaver Lake," said Jareth, "I suggest we announce ourselves with a Contact Song this time."

The others agreed, and the four of them raised their voices in a brief howl. Almost immediately they were answered by the pack – not with Pack Song, as might have been expected, but with a Contact Song of their own. This conveyed no rebuff – on the contrary, it invited further interaction. This pack sounded quite hospitable.

"Right," said Baru, "they know we're here. Let's get going."

"No," Kona said firmly, "we'll wait here for them to find us."

They did not have long to wait before the pack arrived, looking rather lean to the Stony Brook wolves, as though they were under-nourished. Since this probably meant they were suffering from a shortage of food, they might have been expected to drive any competitors from their territory at once – yet they were wagging their tails in friendly greeting.

"Welcome to Grassy Hollow, strangers," said a black male, evidently the leader. "My name is Valzir. What do you wish of us?"

"Greetings to you all," responded Kona. "We wish for safe passage through your pack's land, nothing more."

"Ah," said Valzir, "you're searching for a place of your own, are you? Of course you may cross our territory – we'll escort you ourselves. But before we set off, would you like something to eat?

Food here hasn't been abundant lately, as no doubt you can tell from our appearance, but you're welcome to join us in what little there is."

"We would be delighted," said Kona appreciatively. "I must say, we weren't expecting such kindness after the reception we received from the Beaver Lake wolves."

"Oh?" Valzir said. "An unfriendly pack?"

"You could say that," averred Jareth.

Valzir and the rest of the Grassy Hollow pack proceeded to conduct the Stony Brook wolves deeper into their territory, where, in the absence of larger prey, they hunted mice. Each wolf caught several, but they were a mere mouthful, eaten whole. After a rather subdued Hunt Song, Valzir, looking a little ashamed, showed them to a patch of blueberry bushes, where they spent some time dexterously plucking berries from the stems with their teeth. It was a meagre meal and no-one had anywhere near enough, though naturally the Stony Brook wolves did not say so. If this was all the pack had to live on, they were generous indeed to share it.

Later, as they rested on the banks of the stream that ran through Grassy Hollow, Kona told them the tale of his adoption into the Stony Brook pack and of the purpose of the journey he and the others were now making.

"An intriguing tale," commented Valzir. "I admire your courage, all of you, but I must say that I know of no mountains in the direction of the sunset, much less a cold land beyond them. I fear you may have a long way to go."

"We're prepared for that," Baru assured him, "and for anything we might meet on the way."

"Don't be so sure," warned Valzir. "You may encounter things you never saw with your birth pack."

"When we were cubs," said Baru, "our parents, and the rest of the pack, gave us descriptions of all the creatures and situations we might ever come across – even those that had never occurred in Stony Brook."

"I don't doubt it," Valzir answered, "but that doesn't mean you're prepared to face them. You're a brave wolf, Baru – I can see that – but there are some things in the world that are too much for any wolf."

Baru dismissed this with a confident: "We'll see."

Valzir, wanting to keep the peace, said no more on the subject and shifted the conversation towards other things. Presently, he asked his guests if they were ready to move on.

"We're ready when you are, Valzir," Kona cheerfully replied. "There's no particular hurry."

As it turned out, it took them three days to traverse the pack's territory. During this time they ate nothing but a few more berries, but wolves can fast for many days if need be and none of them complained of hunger. They said their goodbyes at the small hills that formed the boundary of Grassy Hollow, and the Stony Brook wolves departed feeling encouraged by the friendliness of the wolves they left behind. It gave them new heart after the discovery of the bones in the wood and the hostility of the Beaver Lake pack. Their journey had not begun auspiciously, but with the parting howls of the Grassy Hollow pack ringing in their ears, even Jareth was inclined to think that the remainder of the way might not, after all, be so bad.

11
The Hunting of the Moose

The moon waxed and waned, and as the days passed and the nights grew longer, the wolves noticed a decided nip in the air, particularly in the early mornings, which spoke of the arrival of autumn, and the promise of winter not far behind. A forest became visible on the horizon, its falling leaves a riot of browns, reds and yellows, and as they made towards it the wind brought to their questing noses the tantalizing scent of moose. Soon, they caught sight of the herd, emerging from the trees and heading in their direction.

"It looks like the food shortage in Grassy Hollow will soon be over," Shimook remarked.

"And the food shortage in our stomachs," said Baru. "We haven't had a decent meal since leaving Stony Brook."

"You mean you want to hunt one of them, Baru?" asked Jareth timidly.

"Of course."

"But we've never hunted moose without the pack's help."

"And now's the perfect time to start."

"Kona, what do you think?" Shimook interjected.

Kona studied the herd. It was true that they had never hunted such large prey without the help of their elders, but it was also true that they had to start sooner or later. Then again, such a hunt could be very dangerous. His stomach rumbled. Baru was right in that they had not eaten particularly well since leaving Stony Brook, and the sight and scent of the moving mountains of meat made his mouth water.

"I don't know, Shimook," he said. "It would be risky, but ... perhaps if we go a bit closer some sort of opportunity might present itself."

They continued towards the herd and, as they drew nearer, perceived that the moose were not as vigilant as they should have been and had not seen the wolves. Autumn was their breeding season, and there was conflict within the group. The antlers of the bulls, which had been growing since shortly after previous set were cast during last winter, had reached their full size, and had recently shed the layer of skin, called 'velvet', that had provided them with nourishment as they grew. On some of the bulls, this could be seen hanging in tatters from the newly-exposed bone. They were now ready for combat.

The focus of the herd's attention was its dominant bull, an enormous beast whose great antlers spanned a length beyond that of a wolf's body, and a slightly smaller bull, with smaller though still impressive antlers, who appeared to be challenging his authority.

The wolves sat down and watched. The two bulls faced each other, pawing the ground with their front hooves and tossing their heads menacingly. Then the dominant bull let out a tremendous bellow and charged, head down, at his rival. Their antlers crashed together with a booming crack, like that of thunder, and the smaller bull was hurtled backwards by the impact. But he immediately threw himself forward again, and they stood with antlers interlocked, each straining against the other as he strove to push his opponent back.

This went on for some time, and before long the wolves noticed that the larger bull was tiring. He was old, they realized, and despite his size and experience he could not stand up against such a determined rival for much longer.

They separated and the old bull, breathing heavily now, charged again. But the challenger, instead of meeting his rush head-on, twisted away and came in from the side, his antlers striking at the other's flank. The elder staggered, and the wolves saw that he had been gored. He was bleeding from several deep wounds where the tines of his rival's antlers had penetrated his flesh, and retreated when the other advanced. It was plain that the battle was won.

The herd gathered behind the victorious bull and, following meekly in his wake, filed past their erstwhile leader, who remained where he was, watching them go. His reign was over.

"Come on!" cried Baru, jumping up. "His loss is our gain!"

He began to run towards the injured bull. On seeing him coming, the moose gave an alarmed snort and then, too tired from his fight to flee, lowered his head, preparing to defend himself from this new threat. As the wolf drew closer, he swung his antlers at him. Kona's short, sharp bark of warning came too late, and Baru was bowled over by the blow.

Kona remembered vividly the voice of Annik, back in Stony Brook when they were still cubs, saying: "The wolf who attacks the moose alone is either very brave, very foolish, or very hungry."

Baru, he thought, was all three. But there was no time for reflection now. If the moose struck again Baru would probably be killed. Kona, with Shimook beside him, ran forward. Jareth, afraid, hung back, but the two wolves were enough to distract the moose. He left Baru lying where he had fallen and charged them. They parted, one dashing to each side, and Kona glimpsed Baru getting to his paws, winded but otherwise unharmed.

The moose tried to trample Shimook, stamping with his huge hooves, and Kona, seeing an advantage, sprang in and sank his teeth into the creature's pendulous nose. The moose's head was pulled down by his weight and Shimook at once went for the throat, but the moose jerked his head up again, lifting Kona clear off the ground. Dangling in the air, he clung on tenaciously as the moose tried to dislodge him by violently shaking his head.

Baru, having recovered, returned to the fray, jumping up and tearing at the moose's injured flank. He did not hang on, but released his grip at once and ran round to the moose's other side, again attacking the flank. The moose, not only weary but rapidly losing blood from his wounds, was weakening. His head drooped, and Kona's paws regained contact with the earth.

"Now, Jareth!" Shimook called out.

Jareth approached with some trepidation, looking rather helplessly to her sister for further instructions. Shimook shouted: "Get one of its hind legs!"

Jareth summoned her courage and obeyed, her teeth closing on the moose's left hind leg. Then Shimook went for the right front leg. The moose tried to shake them off, lost his balance and fell. Kona loosed his hold on the nose and clamped his jaws around the throat, shutting off the moose's breath. Already panting and exhausted from the two long struggles of the day, the beast died in moments.

The wolves stepped back from their kill, Jareth saying excitedly: "We did it! We brought down a moose, all by ourselves!"

"I knew we could," replied Baru, with more than a hint of pride. He grinned round at them all. "It'll take us *days* to finish this! Days!"

The others grinned back, sharing his delight in their achievement, and then, as one, the four of them lifted their voices in a full-throated Hunt Song. Just as they drew to a close, they caught sight of another wolf trotting towards them across the plain.

"Have we hunted in another pack's territory again?" asked Jareth, thinking nervously of Beaver Lake.

"He seems to be alone," Shimook observed.

"He might have been sent to investigate us," said Baru. "The rest of the pack could be hiding in the forest."

"But we didn't find any scent marks," said Kona.

Then, before anyone could say anything more, the wolf reached them.

"Greetings to you," he said, wagging his tail, "and congratulations on your kill!"

"Who are you?" said Baru suspiciously. "Is the rest of your pack nearby?"

"My name is Neeko," answered the newcomer, "and I left my pack some time ago. I'm a lone wolf."

"Oh? Why did you leave?"

"I just felt like I needed to get out on my own," said Neeko, showing no concern at Baru's brusque manner. "Do some travelling, see something of the world. I've been wandering in this area for a while now. I happened to witness the last part of your hunt, and I was wondering whether you might be so kind as to let me join you."

Since there was more than enough food for all of them, even Baru could not reasonably object to this, and they agreed. They wasted no more time on talking, turning their attention instead to the great feast before them.

12
An Unnatural Death

When the Stony Brook wolves were ready to move on, Neeko went with them. Lately he had begun to tire of being on his own, and, having heard their story, was as intrigued by their quest and as impressed with their courage as the Grassy Hollow pack had been. No-one had any objection to his joining them, and he was soon to prove himself useful.

The five of them reached the forest two days after they left the remains of the moose. As soon as they entered it they knew something was amiss. That they could see no other creatures was not particularly unusual, but that they could hear no other creatures was. A forest is usually full of the noises of its inhabitants going about their business, but here there was only the wind in the trees, eerily loud without other sounds to go with it.

It was not that there were no animals in the forest – there were, for the wolves could smell them. But there was fear in the air and the animals were keeping still and silent in hope that the cause of it would pass them by.

The wolves were troubled but, since there was nothing else for them do to, they kept going. The mood of the forest infected them, however, and they went cautiously, keeping under cover and making as little noise as possible. Presently, the wind brought to them a new scent – the scent of some animal, but one they had never smelled before. There was something about it that filled them with dread. They had no doubt that it was the scent of whatever had cast its fearful spell over the forest.

"I think we should go back," said Jareth vehemently. "I don't want to be anywhere near something that smells like that."

The others thought the same, but Baru, who hated to admit to himself that the scent made him as nervous as his sister, said: "We have to go through this forest. If we turn back now, we'll only have to come back later, and I'm sure we can avoid whatever it is that scent belongs to. I say we keep going."

He looked at each of them in turn, as though challenging them to confess to cowardice. One by one, all rather unwillingly, they agreed with him. They continued. Soon they were approaching a clearing and, not wanting to go into the open without first making sure it was safe, they went carefully up to it and crouched in the undergrowth at its edge.

A herd of elk filled the clearing, milling to and fro in agitation. They, like everything else in the forest, could sense danger, and their usual response would have been to run from it. But, not knowing exactly where it was, they did not know which way to run, and were working themselves into a frenzy.

Then, on the other side of the clearing, the wolves caught sight of another creature concealing itself in the undergrowth, watching the elk. It was not a creature they knew, but they recognized it instantly as the source of the fear in the forest and the frightening scent. Like an angry bear, it stood on its hind legs, and it was holding something which resembled a long stick in its front paws. It had an odd, flat face, mostly hairless, and its hide hung in loose folds around it as though not part of its body at all. In itself it did not look particularly threatening, yet it exuded menace and the promise of violence in a manner that was as bewildering as it was horrifying. There was something not right, not *natural* about it – it did not belong here with the wolves and the elk and the myriad other animals with which they shared their environment. It was somehow fundamentally different from all of them, leading an entirely separate existence from the one they knew. It was something not part of their world – an interloper, an alien, an intruder in a realm where it had no place. It terrified the wolves, and they wanted at once to put as much distance between it and themselves as they could.

The Stony Brook wolves were in the act of turning to flee (even Baru did not attempt to conceal his fear now), when they were checked by Neeko's sudden, urgent command: "Don't run! Keep still!"

"*Don't* run?" hissed Shimook. "Why not?"

"We're too close," Neeko explained, as they sank back into reluctant crouches. "If we run now, it'll see us, and if it sees us it will kill us without a second thought."

Though there was no obvious reason for the creature to wish to kill them, none of them doubted for a moment that it would. On some subconscious level, they had known as soon as they set eyes on it that its purpose here was death.

"It won't notice us if we don't move," Neeko went on. "It's concentrating on the elk – it must be hunting them. So keep still, all of you, and ... and we might get out of this alive."

"But what ... what ... what *is* it?" gulped Jareth, almost choking on her fright.

"It's a human," said Neeko. He was trembling. "I should have known, I suppose, from the scent and the fear. But I'd only heard about them – I've never actually seen one before. I hoped I never would."

"Well, we've never even heard of them," said Baru. "Our pack never mentioned them to us – they must be outside their experience."

"Then they're lucky," said Neeko shortly. "Now, from what I've been told, it will point that stick at the elk it wants, there will be a loud bang, and the elk will fall down, dead. When the bang comes, we'll want to run even more than we do now, but we *mustn't* move. If we move, we die."

As he finished speaking, the human raised its stick and pointed it at the dominant bull of the herd. The wolves were surprised – this was the very last animal any normal predator would target, since it was the largest and fittest member of the herd and, thus, would be the most difficult to bring down.

Then the bang Neeko had spoken of ripped through the silence of the forest. It was by sheer effort of will against every screaming instinct to run that the five wolves forced themselves to stay where they were. They pressed hard against each other, trying to hold each other steady as their legs jerked spasmodically, quivering with the desire to carry them as far as possible from that terrible creature and its noise. The elk, now completely panic-stricken, burst into flight, bolting in every direction. Except for the bull. He lay motionless in the now empty clearing, bleeding from a great wound in one side. Somehow – none of the wolves knew how – the human had killed without ever touching its victim.

It stepped into the clearing and, putting its stick aside, bent over its kill. All predators the wolves knew had some manner of paying their respects to their prey and sending its soul to the Otherworld after a successful hunt – some by uttering a particular cry (though few were so eloquent as their own Hunt Song), some by speaking ritual words, some with a certain method of touching the body or marking the ground. They expected the human to do something like this, but instead it produced a long, pointed thing that caught the light and, holding this in its right front paw, began hacking at the carcass. The wolves were shocked and appalled by the disrespect it showed for the fellow being whose life it had taken.

Somewhere, in a detached part of his mind, Kona realized that, with the human absorbed in its task, they could probably now creep away unnoticed. But he could not move. He was paralysed with terror, and his companions were the same. They could only watch, aghast, as the human proceeded to cut off the elk's head. This done, it retrieved its stick and, clutching the severed head by the antlers, walked away. For a long time the wolves remained still and silent, anticipating its return. When it became clear that it was not coming back, they very gradually began to relax. Eventually, Kona found his voice. "Isn't it going to eat the elk?" he asked Neeko, perplexed by the human's behaviour.

"No," Neeko replied in a low voice. "It didn't kill the elk for food, but for fun. Alone among all animals, humans kill simply because they enjoy it."

The Stony Brook wolves stared at him, open-mouthed, hardly able to believe what they were hearing. As predators themselves, they understood and accepted killing for food as a perfectly natural process. That was the role allocated to them by the Great Spirit. They understood, too, that it was sometimes necessary for creatures to kill each other for different reasons, such as for a mate or territory. But to kill solely for the pleasure of killing – they were overcome with horror and disgust at the thought.

"They believe themselves superior to all other animals," Neeko continued, "and think that gives them the right to kill whenever and whatever they wish, for no other purpose than that they feel like it."

"But that's ... bizarre," said Kona. "Surely they remember what the Great Spirit told us in the Dawn Time, that no one creature can survive without all the others, and so we are all equally important?"

"It's said they turned their backs on the Great Spirit long ago," answered Neeko, "and that they live now by laws of their own making, rather than those of nature. And they hate wolves. They have killed thousands upon thousands of us, even exterminating us from some areas. Apparently, they think us vicious, despite the fact that no healthy wolf has ever attacked them. Only wolves with the foaming-mouth madness have done so, and they can hardly be blamed."

The Stony Brook wolves had heard of this nightmarish disease, though fortunately had never encountered a sufferer themselves. It made animals froth at the mouth and drove them to insanity – an insanity which caused abnormal aggression, making an infected individual attack anything that moved. An animal bitten by such a one would itself become infected. They could well believe that only a wolf so afflicted would dare attack a creature like the one they had seen – any sane wolf would run in the opposite direction.

"They've killed all those wolves, and they think *us* vicious?" Baru cried, half in outrage and half in astonishment.

"That's what I've heard, yes. And the crazy thing is, some of them must know we aren't. There's a tale in my pack – my former pack, I should say – that tells of how one spring, back before my parents' parents were born, a human came to our territory and crawled into the birthing den. The alpha pair were inside with their new litter. They must have been desperate to get away, but there was only one way in and out of the den, and the human was blocking it. Then the human seized one of the cubs. As you know, almost all animals will attack to protect their offspring, and if it had been anything but a human molesting their cubs, the parents would certainly have done so. But they were so afraid of the human that they cringed at the back of the den while it made off with the cub. I can't imagine what it wanted it for. But anyway, I'm sure we'd all have done the same in their position, and it must have shown that human, at least, how little inclination we have to attack them."

Nobody spoke for a while. Then Shimook, indicating the fallen elk with a tilt of her head, said: "We should do something to help his soul on to the Otherworld, since the human did nothing. Perhaps the Death Song?"

"The Death Song is for wolves, not prey," said Baru.

"The Hunt Song, then."

"But it's not our kill."

Kona, emerging from cover with some trepidation, went to the poor, mutilated body and briefly pressed his muzzle to its bloody, lifeless side. Had it been the victim of any other predator, the wolves would gladly have scavenged from the carcass, but to eat from something killed with such contempt seemed so wrong that not one of them even considered it.

"I don't know your gods, or your customs," Kona whispered to the elk, "but I ask Alpha-he and Alpha-she, the father and mother of my kind, to guide you to the Otherworld, and grant you peace."

"Well said, Kona," Neeko approved.

"Neeko, why did the human take the elk's head?" Jareth asked him, with a shudder.

"Who knows?" said Neeko. "Now come, let's get away from here."

The wolves departed hurriedly from that horrible scene of unnatural death. None of them would ever forget what they had witnessed that day.

13
The River and Beyond

The following day, they left the forest behind them. They were glad to be out of it, for even when the normal activities of the animals resumed after the departure of the human, the noises they made had seemed somehow muted, subdued, as though they were afraid the human would hear them and return. The wolves themselves were still wary, and everywhere they looked they seemed to see an image of the dead, decapitated elk, killed on a whim. Such death for the sake of death alone was most disturbing.

Out on the plain once more, the image faded and they started to feel better – largely because they had something else to think about. The horizon was now dominated by a mountain range, including two gigantic peaks, side by side, that towered over their fellows like an alpha pair over a litter of cubs. These were obviously the Great Peaks of which Rishala had spoken, and the wolves were excited to think that they were within sight of their goal. But they were soon to discover that there would be more obstacles to overcome before they reached it.

As dusk began to fall several days later, they found themselves on the bank of a river. It was wide and deep, the current tearing at a furious pace over a bed of large, irregular rocks, some of which pierced the surface. The rushing water made an ominous, sibilant sound.

"We shall have to cross it," said Kona decisively.

"I was afraid you were going to say that," groaned Jareth.

"We'll wait until morning, of course," he added.

"Oh, of course. That's very reassuring," Jareth said sarcastically.

"Jareth!" said Shimook reproachfully, and her sister, with a rather ashamed expression, looked away.

Kona sat apart for a time after this exchange, watching the sun set. As it sank behind the mountains it turned them into a great, dark, rugged silhouette against a blood-red sky. The scene stirred something in the shadows of his subconscious and, that night, he dreamed again the dream he had had the night Garrin told him the tale of his birth and adoption – the dream of Stony Brook transformed into the snowy wastes of the land beyond the mountains.

Kona rose early the next day, before the others were awake, and, going to the river's edge, bent to drink from the racing water. It was very cold, and he at once began to worry about the crossing. Wolves are good swimmers and are fond of water under normal circumstances, enjoying playing in calm or shallow places. But this was a far more daunting prospect. The current could smash a wolf against the rocks, causing injury, and potentially suck him beneath the surface to his doom. However, the fact was they had no choice. They had to cross if they were to continue their journey. He decided that the best thing to do was to get it over with as soon as possible and, with this thought in mind, roused the others. Soon, all five wolves were standing on the bank.

"I don't like this at all, Kona," said Jareth pessimistically. "I'm sure we'll be drowned, or cut to pieces on the rocks. Or both."

"No, we won't," Kona assured her, sounding much more confident than he felt. "We'll all go together, and then if anyone gets into difficulty, the others will be there to help. Ready?"

"As ready as I'll ever be, I suppose," replied Jareth gloomily and, without further ado, they plunged into the river.

There was an instant shock of cold as the water penetrated their fur, followed by the pull of the current. Knowing it was pointless to try and resist, they allowed themselves to be swept downstream whilst striking out for the opposite bank. Kona, whose big paws made for efficient paddling, made good headway and was soon ahead of the others. His eyes fixed on the bank, he kept his ears tuned to the progress of his companions, hearing an occasional yelp as one or another of them scraped against a rock. He was starting to feel numb from the cold by the time he reached the shallows and scrambled ashore.

Safely on dry land, he shook himself vigorously, both to rid his coat of water and to warm himself up. Looking back at the river, he saw that the others were not far behind him. Neeko was next to reach the bank, followed by Shimook and then Baru. Jareth was the last to crawl out of the water, shivering and exhausted. They shook themselves, as Kona had done, and then all five of them moved away from the river to rest and allow the sun to soak up the remaining moisture from their fur.

A short time later, they continued on their way, making for the forest that lay below the mountain range. They reached it late that afternoon and, inclined to be cautious after their encounter with the human, entered it warily. They soon detected the scent marks of a pack of wolves – eight in all, five female and three male. They announced themselves with a Contact Song, but, receiving no answer, set off into the forest.

Presently they crossed the trail of one of the pack males. The trail was fresh, indicating that he had been there not long before, so they decided to follow it and attempt to catch up with him. He seemed to be searching for something, moving back and forth in a methodical manner, his trail becoming fresher still the further they went. The scent of blood brought them up short, and they began to go more carefully. They came upon the wolf quite suddenly. He lay on the ground in a pool of his own blood, one side ripped open so that the ribs peeped through the ragged flesh. His throat had been torn out with such violence that his head was almost severed from his neck. Though he was approaching his full size, it was clear that he was a juvenile, born only that spring.

The five wolves simply stood, staring at the corpse. That wolf had been alive just moments ago, they were sure of it. Something had killed him, and killed him brutally, while they themselves had been following his trail.

"By Alpha-she's teeth and tail!" gasped Jareth in horror.

"What could have done this?" Baru wondered.

Kona forced himself to take a step towards the body. No tracks were visible on the leaf-strewn forest floor, but as he had suspected the scent of the killer lingered. He did not recognize it. With a motion of his head, he beckoned silently for the others to come and smell for themselves. Naturally, Shimook, Baru and Jareth did not recognize the scent either, but Neeko did. He said: "It's a puma."

The Stony Brook wolves looked at each other. This creature had, of course, been described to them by the pack when they were cubs, and each of them was remembering what they had been told – that the puma, also known as the cougar or mountain lion, is a fearsome predator, capable of killing alone the animals that they must hunt in packs, and that, because the two species compete for the same prey, they are seldom found in the same area.

"Perhaps it killed this wolf to reduce the competition for food," said Kona quietly.

"Yes, I should think so," Neeko agreed.

"You ... you don't think it might still be close, do you?" asked Jareth, looking apprehensively around her.

The thought occurred to them all simultaneously that the puma might indeed still be close – perhaps close enough to be observing them as they spoke. And each of them felt a creeping sensation come over them, as though they were being watched by terrible, unseen eyes.

14
The Whispering Wolves

They left the poor dead wolf, and went further into the forest. They did not run, because they had no wish to make a noise which might draw attention to themselves, but they moved hastily, with many a furtive glance around them, their ears and noses continually scanning their surroundings for sound or scent of approaching danger.

They had not gone far when they heard the swish of undergrowth as something moved through it. They stopped and tried to catch the scent of whatever was approaching, but it was downwind of them, and they were unable to smell it. Then, as it came nearer, they heard the patter of trotting paws – wolf paws. They barely had time to feel relief before the wolf, a nervous-looking female the same age as the dead male, appeared from between two tree trunks. She stopped and stared at them without speaking.

"We come in peace," said Neeko diplomatically. "We're merely passing through and mean no harm to you or your pack. Might I ask your name?"

In a very low voice, as though she was afraid of being overheard, the wolf said: "I am called Zari. You are welcome here, but this is ... not a safe place."

"We know that," said Baru.

"Then you met my brother?" Zari inquired, still in a whisper.

"Your brother?" said Kona, looking round at his companions and seeing his own grim thoughts reflected in their eyes.

"Yes. When we heard you howl, he wanted to come out and look for you, but our father, the leader of our pack, said it was too dangerous. But he went anyway, and since no-one's supposed to go out by themselves, I came to find him. And here *you* are. So I suppose you already met him, and he's gone back to the pack?"

This last was an anxious question, rather than a statement.

"We ... we found a body," Shimook told her awkwardly.

Zari's legs crumpled under her and she collapsed with a little moan. They could not help noticing that, despite her obvious grief, she did not seem surprised – it was almost as though she had been anticipating such news.

"He should not have gone!" she whimpered piteously. "He should not have gone!"

"Um ... perhaps *we* shouldn't be here either," ventured Jareth.

Zari looked wildly round, then drew a deep breath and pulled herself to her paws.

"You're right," she said. "I'll take you to the pack."

They followed Zari for some distance through the trees, until they came to a hole in the ground, from which came the distinct scent of wolves.

"This is where we live, except when we have to hunt," she whispered.

"You *live* underground?" said Baru in amazement.

"Yes. It's not so strange, really – we all spent our first days underground, after all."

The Stony Brook wolves and Neeko were too astonished to say anything more as she led them into the hole. They found themselves in a low, narrow tunnel that sloped downwards into darkness. The day vanished behind them as they proceeded deeper into the earth, arriving finally in a chamber large enough to comfortably accommodate them all. The musty smell of abandonment that pervaded it told the visitors it had not been used for some time, but there was an eerie, expectant feel about it, as though, long deserted as it was, it was still waiting for the return of someone who was never coming back.

Here, Zari left them while she went to fetch the leader of the pack. She returned with both her father, Galtag, and her mother, Wyanath. Though clearly distraught at the loss of their son, which Zari had described to them, they greeted the visitors in a friendly manner. However, Kona and the others were puzzled by the fact that the alpha pair seemed every bit as nervous as their daughter, whom they had assumed from her demeanour to be the omega wolf of her pack, and that, like her, they spoke only in whispers.

"We're so sorry about your son," said Shimook with great sympathy. "If you would allow it, we would be honoured to join the Death Song."

"There will be no Death Song," murmured Galtag. "There are no songs among the whispering wolves."

"The whispering wolves?" said Baru. "Why *do* you whisper all the time?"

60

"We don't like to speak too loudly in case the puma hears us," Wyanath explained, "and we never howl any more. That's why we didn't answer you when *you* howled. You're lucky you didn't attract it when you did that, you know."

"How long have you been living like this?" asked Kona softly.

"It was many seasons ago that it first arrived in our territory," said Galtag. "It began to pick us off one by one, so I made it a rule that no-one was to go around alone, or give away their position by howling or speaking loudly. And then, one night, it attacked us while we slept. It was after that that those of us who survived took to living underground, digging out these tunnels and chambers from our original birthing den. We don't really need to whisper when we're in here – it couldn't get in even if it heard us – but it's become a habit, you see."

"Surely this puma can't fight the whole pack?" said Baru. "Why don't you attack it, all together, and kill it?"

"You saw my son's body," Galtag replied morosely. "I don't doubt that it was horribly maimed. So you have seen what it can do. How could I ask my wolves to face that? And, even if we did succeed in killing it, some of us would assuredly lose our lives before the deed was done. It isn't worth the risk."

"But what about when you hunt?" said Jareth. "Doesn't it come after you then?"

It was Wyanath who answered. She stood out more clearly than the others in the darkness, as she was almost completely white, with only a splash of grey across her lower back. "Yes," she said, "sometimes. We stay as close to the holes as we can on a hunt, and if the puma appears we simply run for cover. And when we make a kill, we dismember it and take it underground with us, so it can't catch us while we're feeding. Actually, we killed yesterday – you may eat, if you're hungry."

"That's very kind," said Shimook. "We *would* like something to eat."

"You take them, Zari," Galtag instructed his daughter. "When you return, we will talk again."

Zari led them out of the chamber and through what seemed a maze of tunnels, until they reached a second chamber. Here, the carcass of a mule deer – in several pieces, and partially consumed – awaited them. Zari told them to eat all they liked, which they thankfully did.

61

When they had finished, Zari showed them back to their chamber, where Galtag and Wyanath were waiting for them.

"Perhaps," Galtag said politely, "you can now tell us something about yourselves, and how you came to be here."

Obligingly, Kona recounted who they were, where they had come from, and why they were there. As he described how Rishala had fled from the wolves of a rival pack, as she had told Garrin, who had told him, Galtag began to mutter to himself: "Yes. Yes, it all fits."

"What?" said Kona, breaking off his tale. "What was that?"

"Your mother," Galtag replied, "this Rishala – I believe she passed through here on her flight."

Kona did not really know why this surprised him. Of course, when he thought about it, she must have come through this forest after she crossed the mountains, on her way to the wood where Garrin had found her.

"Go on," he said.

"Well," continued Galtag, "several seasons ago – it would have been shortly before you were born – we picked up the trail of a female wolf crossing our territory, coming from the direction of the mountains. She must have been in a hurry, because we did not find any places where she'd stopped to rest. We followed her trail to the edge of the forest, but saw no reason to go any further."

"So you think she was Rishala?" said Kona quietly.

"It would certainly seem so, yes."

"There was no-one chasing her? No wolves from this rival pack she talked about?"

"Not that I know of, but it would explain why she was in such a hurry if she thought she was being pursued."

"They must have given up the chase, but left her thinking they were still coming after her," said Kona thoughtfully, "otherwise she wouldn't have kept going all the way to Stony Brook. Or nearly all the way."

"I suppose not," agreed Galtag. "But we can discuss this further tomorrow – it's late now, and time we all slept. We will leave you."

The three whispering wolves departed, and Kona, Shimook, Jareth and Neeko made themselves comfortable on the floor of the chamber. Baru, however, would not lie down, and kept pacing to and fro, disturbing the others.

"What is it, Baru?" asked Shimook at last.

"It's *this*," Baru answered, indicating the chamber with a jerk of his head. "Wolves skulking underground like rabbits. It isn't right."

"Perhaps you should go and sleep outside, then," suggested Neeko. He had, of course, intended this jocularly, but Baru, his pride hurt by what he perceived as lack of faith in his courage, took him seriously.

"I will, by the Alphas!" he snapped. "*I'm* not afraid to behave like a real wolf!"

So saying, he marched out of the chamber and up the tunnel that led to the surface. Alarmed, the others went after him and tried to persuade him to come back underground. Unfortunately, Baru was now determined to prove himself and would not be talked round. Neither would he hear of them remaining outside with him. Eventually, reluctant though they were to leave him there alone (or indeed at all), they had no choice but to return to the chamber without him and hope that the puma would not come to their part of the forest that night.

15
The Puma

Kona woke with a start, an inexplicable feeling of impending disaster coursing through him. He sat up, peering about him. He was unable to see much in the dim chamber, but the steady, rhythmic breathing of his companions told him they were still asleep. He was about to lie down again when the howl of a wolf rent the night. It was Baru's Contact Song, but it was distorted almost beyond recognition by a note Kona had never heard before from his adoptive brother – the note of terror. The next moment, the howl was drowned out by a thunderous roar.

The other wolves were awake on the instant.

"What was that?" said Jareth.

"I don't know," replied Kona, struggling to keep the fear he felt out of his voice. "It sounded like Baru ..."

"And the puma," Jareth finished for him, in a tone of utter panic.

"We've got to help him!" cried Shimook, dashing into the tunnel.

"I'll go and find the pack," said Neeko, leaving the chamber by the tunnel Galtag, Wyanath and Zari had taken earlier. Kona followed Shimook up to the surface, Jareth rather reluctantly tagging along behind him.

As the three Stony Brook wolves arrived in the forest, Galtag emerged from another hole nearby and rushed over to them.

"Come back underground!" he whispered urgently. "There's nothing you can do for him now."

"We have to try," said Kona resolutely. "Where is Neeko?"

"Underground, in your chamber," Galtag replied. "I told him to go back and stay there when he came to tell us what you were doing. I'm going back now, and you'll come with me if you value your lives."

Before any of them could say another word, Baru's terrified howl rang out again. It was closer than before, and more desperate. Galtag disappeared back down the hole.

The sound of running paws was audible now, and Kona, Shimook and Jareth knew Baru – and, no doubt, the puma – would soon be upon them. In an agony of expectant dread, they waited. It felt like several life-times before Baru burst through the undergrowth. He was in the final stages of exhaustion, his tongue lolling from his open, panting mouth, his eyes so glazed that he did not appear to see the wolves standing in front of him.

Clearly, he did not realize that safety lay just ahead, for instead of making for the hole behind them, he staggered to a halt and turned to confront his pursuer. It took only a heart-beat for the others to guess his intention. Baru was preparing to make his last stand. Proud to the end, he was determined to die fighting, not running.

Then the undergrowth parted a second time, and the puma stepped into view. A collective gasp that was part horror and part awe escaped the watching wolves. They could recognize and respect a master hunter when they saw one, and this was a beast as magnificent as it was terrible, something to be admired even as they feared it. The wolves stood a little taller, due to the length of their legs, but the puma was longer, heavier and much more powerfully built. Huge muscles rolled beneath its rich tan pelt as it glided towards them on silent paws, moving with an effortless grace that spoke of the kind of agility a wolf could only envy. It growled – a rumbling, guttural growl – and bared the most fearsome set of teeth the wolves had ever seen, or imagined in their nightmares.

The puma fixed its unblinking gaze on Baru. He seemed almost to wilt before that baleful glare, and, though he tried to out-stare it, he was compelled to look away. And then it struck. Rearing up on its hind legs, it lashed out with one fore-paw. The cruel, curved claws caught the moonlight and flashed faintly in the night. Unlike those of wolves, which were permanently extended and therefore blunt from being constantly worn down against the ground, the puma's claws were retractile – kept sheathed within the paws until the animal wished to use them, they remained sharp and deadly.

The blow hit Baru on the right side of his head, raking across his cheek and down his muzzle, tearing open deep, parallel wounds as it went. Baru, spun round by the impact, had time for a single yelp of pain before he collapsed, unconscious.

The other three wolves moved simultaneously. Jareth, sure that her brother was done for, bolted for subterranean sanctuary. Shimook, keeping her eyes on the puma, ran to Baru and gently started to lick the blood from his face. Kona bounded forward and stood protectively in front of them.

The advancing puma showed no concern. It continued towards them, step by inexorable step. Two more wolves meant nothing to it. If they did not get out of its way, it would kill them along with their fallen companion.

"Shimook?" said Kona, without looking round.

"Yes?"

"Get Baru underground. Now."

"But what are you ...?"

"I'm going to distract it," he hissed, keeping his voice low despite the unlikelihood of the puma understanding their language.

"*What*? But Kona ..."

"Do as I say!"

The command snapped out with an authority that brooked no arguments. Shimook took Baru by the scruff of his neck and began dragging him towards the hole behind her. The puma, seeing its victim about to be rescued, let out an angry growl and hastened forward. Kona, snarling as fiercely as he could, blocked its path. Just before it raised a paw to knock him aside, he seemed to sense its intent and leapt clear. However, instead of coming after him, it charged once more towards Shimook and Baru.

Kona could think of only one thing to do. As the puma passed him, he lunged in and sank his teeth into its haunch. A roar of mingled surprise and rage broke from the beast as it whirled round. Kona had already let go and darted out of range, but he had its full attention now and it surged towards him. He did not wait to meet it, but turned tail and fled into the forest. Knowing few predators can resist chasing something that runs away from them, he trusted that the puma's hunting instinct would draw it after him.

Shimook watched in amazement as wolf and puma vanished among the trees. Kona had given her the time she needed to get Baru and herself underground, but his daring attack on the puma had shocked her into immobility. Then it occurred to her that at any moment the beast might abandon its pursuit and return. Backing into the hole, she pulled the limp form of Baru after her down the tunnel and into the chamber. There, she found a quaking Jareth in the company of Neeko and Galtag.

"Where's Kona?" asked Jareth. "What happened?"

"He drew it off," answered Shimook, still slightly dazed by what she had seen.

"He did *what?*" exclaimed Neeko.

"He drew it off," Shimook repeated. "He attacked it and made it chase him so that I could help Baru."

Jareth and Neeko gaped speechlessly at each other. Shimook resumed cleaning Baru's wounds.

"He will be killed," said Galtag with sad certainty. "What was he thinking?"

"He was thinking of us," Shimook replied.

16
Alone in the Dark

A short while later, Baru regained consciousness. Blinking dizzily, he looked up into the anxious faces of his companions and then, rather unsteadily, got to his paws. A trickle of blood ran down his muzzle from one of his wounds, which had almost stopped bleeding thanks to the attentions of Shimook. He winced as he licked it away.

"Can you tell us what happened?" Neeko asked him.

"I was asleep," said Baru, "outside, where you left me. I woke up, and the puma was ... there. Between me and the hole. It was just about to pounce. So I ran."

He hung his head, ashamed.

"No-one thinks any less of you for that," Jareth assured him.

"I ran for a long, long time," continued Baru. "I howled for help, but I didn't think anyone would come to my aid, even if anyone could hear me. Eventually, I couldn't run any more. I decided that, since I was to die anyway, I would do so with my teeth buried in that creature's flesh. I turned and faced it, but before I could do anything else, it struck me. And then ... then ... the next thing I remember is waking up here. How did I get here?"

"We did hear you howl," Shimook explained, "and we came outside to try and help you. You must have run in a circle, because you appeared almost immediately. We saw the puma strike you – it happened before we could intervene – and it knocked you unconscious. But we managed to get you underground after that."

"You did?" said Baru, puzzled. "How? And where is Kona?"

When Shimook told him what Kona had done, his jaw dropped. Then, in a very small and uncharacteristic voice, he said: "He saved my life."

"And probably lost his own," said Galtag. He spoke, as always, under his breath, but Baru heard him. His head snapped up in alarm. "He's still out there?" he exclaimed. "He didn't come back?"

"No," said Shimook, and added hastily: "Not yet."

"I thought you meant that ... that he'd drawn it off and then returned. I thought he was off underground somewhere, resting."

"Well ... he's not."

68

"Then why are we sitting about here?" cried Baru. "We must help him! Come on!"

He was heading for the surface before the others could move. Galtag's face registered disbelief that a wolf who had once encountered the puma would voluntarily do so again. Neeko darted round Baru and placed himself in front of the exit tunnel.

"You're injured, Baru," he said reasonably. "You must stay here. I'll go and look for Kona."

Baru opened his mouth to protest, then paused. If he had allowed himself to be persuaded back underground earlier, they would not be in this position now.

"You're right, I suppose," he said reluctantly.

"I'll go with you, Neeko," said Shimook. "Jareth, will you stay here with Baru?"

"Oh, yes, of course I will," Jareth said with some relief. She had been feeling that she ought to offer to go too, much as the prospect terrified her, and was grateful to her sister for providing an excuse for her to stay behind.

***

Kona's plan had been a simple one. After drawing the puma away from Shimook and Baru and keeping it occupied long enough for them to reach safety, he had intended to double back and join them. The puma, however, had other ideas. Having lost its first victim because he had doubled back, it was not about to let this other wolf – this wolf who had dared to attack it – repeat the trick. Each time Kona tried to circle round towards the holes, it cut him off, leaving him with no alternative but to keep running in the opposite direction to his goal and getting further and further away from it as he did so.

At first, he was not too worried about this. He was fleet and fit, and was confident that the prodigious stamina of his kind could outlast that of the puma. True, it had exhausted Baru, but it was surely tired after such a chase and would not be able to run for long. Therefore, he decided that, providing he could avoid being caught in the meantime, all he had to do was to run until it wore itself out, and then return to the others. But as the night drew on and he found himself beginning to tire, a shadow of doubt crossed his mind. The puma showed no sign of tiring, and now he was forced to consider the possibility that it possessed greater stamina than he. The possibility that he might be caught.

His fear of the beast that ran behind him, under control until now, flared up. He had saved his companions, but in doing so he had run himself, quite literally, into the very teeth of danger. What would they do if he was killed? Without him, their journey was pointless.

Kona saw the edge of the forest ahead of him. The boundary of the puma's territory, surely? And surely here it would give up the chase? He dashed past the tree-line and out into open country – the very ground he had covered that day, after crossing the river. He risked a quick glance behind him, hoping to see the puma pulling up at the forest's edge. Instead, he found himself looking straight into its gaping jaws. It was still following him, and worse, it had narrowed the gap between them. It was gaining on him.

He sprang forward with renewed terror, stretching out his stride, but he was panting for breath now, the air rasping in his throat. His lungs burned and his heart was pounding painfully, from fright as much as from exertion. He knew he could not run for much longer, yet to stop meant certain death. It occurred to him that this was how animals such as deer must feel when pursued by wolves, how many times he himself, with the pack, had run his prey to exhaustion to catch it. The hunter had become the hunted. It was a chilling thought.

Eventually, Kona's flight brought him to the river. Now, as he raced along the bank, the effort required to lift his aching limbs again and again was almost more than he could bear. With each bound, he felt sure that the next would be his last, expecting at any moment to feel the puma's claws in his back. He knew it was only a matter of time before his muscles failed him, and when they did, he would be caught. Despair filled him as he realized there was nothing he could do and nobody to come to his rescue. He was alone in the dark with death running close behind him.

"First Alphas, help me!" he prayed silently.

Then, suddenly, he was on to a steep, muddy part of the bank. His fleeing paws, unable to maintain their grip on the slippery surface, slid out from under him. He fell, skidding down towards the river. The water here was a raging torrent, shredded by a multitude of jagged rocks. At the sight of it rushing up to meet him, Kona knew it was all over for him. Either the puma would catch him here on the bank and tear him apart, or he would plunge into that swirling chaos in which, in his present drained state, he would have no hope of survival. He was doomed.

Shimook and Neeko had no trouble locating the trail left by Kona and the puma. They tried not to let themselves think too much about what might have happened as they hastened along it, but it was difficult not to recall Zari's brother. They were terribly afraid, both for Kona and for themselves. Perhaps the puma had killed Kona and was returning, towards them, to seek out his companions. Perhaps it was lying in wait for them somewhere ahead. Perhaps it had given up the chase altogether, and Kona, safe and unhurt, was making his way back to them. Neither of them could quite believe this, but nor could they bring themselves to believe he was dead.

The trail seemed to run in an almost straight line. Occasionally it weaved from side to side, and they deduced that here Kona had attempted to double back and been prevented from doing so by his pursuer. They followed the trail to the edge of the forest and out onto the grassland beyond. The sky was lightening towards dawn before they came once more to the river, surprised at the distance Kona had covered during the night and wondering frantically what it might mean.

They ran along the bank until they came to a steep, muddy place, clearly marked with the paw-prints of Kona and of the puma. And here the trail ceased. Shimook and Neeko stood there in silence as the implications of what they were seeing sank into them. Both Kona and the puma must have fallen into the river. Neeko turned away, but Shimook, overcome with the need to know, to be certain, stepped forwards and peered over the bank.

Two great, deep furrows had been gouged through the mud where the two animals had slithered down towards the river. One, the larger one, continued into the water itself. At the bottom of the other, lying at the very edge of the shallows, was Kona. His eyes were closed, but he did not appear to be injured.

Beyond him lay a particularly wild stretch of the river, where numerous pointed rocks thrust up through the surface like shattered teeth and whipped the churning water into foam – foam which was stained here and there with traces of rapidly-fading red.

Shimook looked downstream just before the current loosened the broken body of the puma from the rocks against which it had been pinned and swept it away round a bend in the river.

17
Across the Mountains

Kona had clung to the slippery bank as tenaciously as he had clung to the moose's nose, digging his paws deep into the mud in a last, desperate attempt to save himself. He had come to a halt just short of the turbulent water, and heard the splash of the puma falling in and its cry of pain as it struck the rocks. He saw it sink, then rise to the surface, bleeding and motionless. Then relief and exhaustion had overwhelmed him, and he lost consciousness. Now, he awoke to Shimook and Neeko licking his face as they tried to revive him. It was morning.

"Are you hurt, Kona?" asked Shimook anxiously.

"No," he replied, rising carefully as he tested each limb in turn. "Luckily for me, the puma fell into the river before it could get hold of me. How is Baru?"

"He'll be fine. His wounds are painful, but not serious."

The steep, muddy bank was too slippery for the wolves to scramble back up, so they made their way along the water's edge, wary of the fierce current, until they found a lower, more gently sloping part of the bank. Kona paused before following Shimook and Neeko up it, snatching a quick drink and silently thanking both the Alphas and the river itself for his deliverance.

On their return to the pack, the whispering wolves stared at Kona as though he had just fallen from the sky, so astonished were they to see him alive and unharmed. They were speechless, unable to express their surprise, and in the silence Baru approached Kona. With head and tail respectfully lowered, he addressed his adoptive brother in a most humble tone.

"I owe you my life, Kona," he said. "I see now that Shimook and Jareth are right to call you leader. And ... and from now onwards, I shall do the same."

Kona was so taken aback that he did not know what to say. Fortunately, Galtag broke the tension. Finding his voice at last, he demanded to know what had happened and how Kona had escaped the puma's wrath. So, with him and the others listening in rapt attention, Kona described the terrible chase through the night, its culmination at the river, and the death of the puma.

Afterwards, Galtag led his pack out of the holes in which they had been forced to hide and they howled in celebration, hardly able to contain their joy at being able to do so without fear.

They remained with Galtag's pack for a time, helping them adjust to a life above ground. At first, they were habitually on guard, periodically glancing over their shoulders and scenting the air, especially when feeding. It was a strange experience for them to eat their prey where it fell, instead of dismembering it and taking it underground as had been their custom. Nor could they manage to abandon their whispering, so established had the habit become, but they soon began to relax and enjoy their new lives. They had skulked in the shadow of the puma for too long, and now that it was gone they exulted in their freedom.

"I can't thank you enough for what you've done," said Galtag to Kona, more than once. "If any of you feel like staying here and joining my pack, you'll be more than welcome."

Baru's wounds healed, though he would always bear the scars, and eventually Kona knew they must continue their journey. When he said as much to the others, Neeko announced that he was not coming with them. He had decided to take up Galtag's offer of joining his pack.

"I've done enough travelling," he said, "and here I've found a pack I can settle down with. I hope you find the same when you reach this land you're going to. May the Alphas watch over you. I'll miss you all very much."

"We'll miss you too, Neeko," said Shimook with feeling. "You've been a good friend to us. We'd never have survived our encounter with the human if it wasn't for you."

Kona, Baru and Jareth agreed whole-heartedly. At last, when all the farewells had been said, the four Stony Brook wolves set off through the forest towards the Great Peaks and the pass between them that would take them through the mountains.

When the ground first began to slope upwards, they were still surrounded by trees. However, as the ascent grew steeper and the soil stonier, these became fewer and fewer, until they were replaced by stunted bushes. Eventually even these petered out, and there was nothing around them but the bare, barren rock. The desolation, the sheer lifelessness of it, was oppressive.

The higher they climbed, the colder it became. There was a hard, biting edge to the air, and each breath exhaled into it became a cloud of vapour blossoming around their muzzles. Some of the boulders they passed were coated with a film of ice.

Presently a fog rolled in, enveloping them in its chill dampness. It was so dense that, beyond about three steps ahead, it appeared impenetrable, making the wolves feel as though they were constantly about to walk into something solid. After some time of this their sense of motion became confused, and it seemed that they remained in one place, pacing on the spot, whilst the fog swirling about them gave an illusion of forward movement.

Suddenly, Kona became aware that Jareth, who had been to his left, was no longer there. Shimook was on his right, and he could just make out the insubstantial form of Baru in front of him. He could not see Jareth near either of them. He tried to locate her by scent, but the fog masked and suppressed odours beneath its heavy wetness, and he could not smell her.

"Jareth?" he said.

"Kona?" Jareth's response came from somewhere behind him.

"Where are you?"

"Ahead of you, I think," he answered. "Come towards my voice."

A moment later, Jareth appeared out of the fog and hurried over to him.

"We must keep closer together," he advised. "We might all have become separated and lost in this fog. I should have thought of that earlier."

After this they made sure they were always in sight of each other, but they were to have another unpleasant surprise that day. They came upon it abruptly as they rounded a massive boulder – a great crevasse, a yawning gash in the mountainside almost obscured by the fog. Baru, still in front, nearly walked into it before he saw it, his paws scrabbling at the edge. He jumped backwards with a startled yelp.

The wolves peered into the crevasse, listening to the stones dislodged by Baru go rattling down into the hidden gullies below. They did not hear them strike the bottom. The crevasse must be very deep – deep enough to swallow four wolves without a trace.

"That was a narrow escape, Baru," said Kona. "It would be all too easy to fall into something like this when we can't really see where we're going. I suggest we don't go any further until the fog clears."

They retreated to what they considered a safe distance from the crevasse and settled down to wait. Dusk fell, and the fog showed no sign of clearing. Since there was no question of their continuing by night, they slept where they were.

The dawn to which they awoke the following day was crisp and clear. A layer of frost had stolen over the ground while they slept, but the fog had vanished as though it had never been. The wolves skirted round the crevasse, giving it a wide berth, and began to climb once more.

Soon they had reached altitudes where the cold was so intense that perpetual snow masked the face of the mountains. It was frozen and firm under their paws, so it did not hinder their progress, but Shimook, Baru and Jareth shivered continually in the bitter cold. Kona, though he felt the drop in temperature, did not shiver and was grateful for his thicker coat.

It took them all that day and half of the next to reach the summit of the pass between the Great Peaks. From here, they had a view of their journey's end, for spread out before and beneath them lay the land they had been travelling towards since leaving Stony Brook. It was a world of white, snow stretching as far as the eye could see into the distance with nothing to break its monotony but the occasional dark patch, which they guessed to be forest. Winter, still some way off in the land they had left behind, was clearly already under way here. It was a bleak, forbidding place, but the four wolves – no longer just a group of vagrants but, as Garrin had said they would be, a pack in their own right – started unerringly down the mountain pass towards it, undaunted.

18
Strangers in the Snow

It took the wolves nearly two days to reach the foot of the mountains. What they chiefly noticed as they descended was that the snow persisted all the way down on this side, rather than being confined to the heights as on the other side. It brought home to them, perhaps more than anything else, that this was a colder land than the one they knew.

It was not so cold, however, as it had been high in the mountains, and the snow here was not frozen solid. As they loped over it in single file, it crunched beneath their paws, melting slightly under their pads and then re-freezing as they advanced, fixing their tracks in place until the next snow fell and buried them. At times Shimook, Baru and Jareth sank up to their shoulders in the drifts, but Kona's large paws allowed him to walk lightly over the top.

They had not been on level ground for long before they came upon another wolf's tracks in the snow. Baru, comparing them to his own, observed: "It was a big wolf that made these prints."

"Was it?" said Kona cryptically.

"Well, wasn't it?" said Baru, a little impatiently.

For answer, Kona placed one of his front paws next to the tracks, and lifted it away again. The mark he made was almost exactly the same size.

"Oh," said Baru, understanding. "Of course."

"There *is* something strange about them, though," said Kona. "They look sort of blurred round the edges."

"That might just be from the snow melting and re-freezing," Shimook suggested.

"Yes, it might," Kona agreed, sniffing at the tracks, "but I'm fairly certain I can smell more than one wolf here. I know snow doesn't hold scent very well, but ..."

He stopped at a sound from somewhere nearby, and, looking up quickly, saw two wolves trotting towards them, one behind the other. For an instant he thought he glimpsed a third wolf, some distance behind the other two, but then it was gone and there were only the two of them, a female in front and a male behind. Both seemed not to feel the cold through their thick fur, and moved easily over the snow on their large paws. They were Kona's kind.

Even as he realized this, Kona realized too that they had managed to approach unnoticed while he and the others had been busy examining the tracks. He silently admonished himself for not keeping a better look-out.

The two came up to the Stony Brook wolves confidently, with an air of being well able to take care of themselves in the event of a fight breaking out. The fact that they were outnumbered did not appear to worry them.

"Greetings," said the female, rather blandly. "Might I ask your business here?"

Kona guessed that she was trying to size them up, find out more about them before making a judgement, and thought it might be prudent if he, too, did not give too much away.

"We've come in search of some wolves," he said, carefully.

"Yes?" she responded. "Any wolves in particular?"

"You may be one of them," said Kona, imitating her enigmatic manner, "for all I know."

Her eyes narrowed suspiciously, and for one beat of his heart he almost expected her to attack. Then she laughed, openly and cheerfully, and said: "I see neither of us is going to learn much this way! Allow me to introduce myself. My name is Nirrao."

She looked round at her thus-far-silent companion as though inviting him to speak. He stared hard at each of the newcomers before saying tersely: "Dargo." The Stony Brook wolves noticed that he spoke with a slur to his voice, and Kona, looking more closely at him, thought his lower jaw seemed slightly misshapen.

"He's a wolf of few words," said Nirrao with a grin at Dargo, which he wryly returned. "We are members of the Great Peaks pack."

"We're pleased to meet you both," said Kona politely. "I'm called Kona, and these are my pack-mates – Shimook, Baru and Jareth."

"You look ... strange, you three," said Nirrao, tilting her head at Kona's adoptive siblings. "Different to any wolves I've ever seen."

"That's because we're from the warmer lands on the other side of the mountains," said Shimook.

"You've come over the mountains?" said Nirrao, with a new respect.

"That's right," said Kona, "and since it's clear now we don't mean each other any harm, I'll tell you why we've come. You may be able to help us. We've come to find wolves who knew a female named Rishala."

"Rishala!" cried Nirrao and Dargo together. They looked stunned. Obviously, the name meant something to them, and it was just as obviously the last thing they had expected to hear.

"Rishala," murmured Nirrao in wonder. "Rishala ..."

"You knew her, then?" Kona said softly.

"Yes," said Nirrao faintly. "Yes, we knew her."

"Nirrao's sister," said Dargo, matter-of-factly.

"But ... but how do *you* know her?" said Nirrao, staring at Kona in confusion. "How *can* you know her?"

Kona opened his mouth, and had Dargo not spoken first the whole story would have poured out of him then and there. But before he could say anything, Dargo cut him short with: "Tashar must hear this. Come."

"Who's Tashar?"

"Our leader. My brother. Rishala's mate."

"So he *is* still alive!"

"Don't tell me you know him, too?" said Nirrao, in a tone that suggested astonishment was about to overwhelm her.

"No, no," smiled Kona, "but it's him we were hoping to meet."

"Then follow me," said Dargo laconically. "Tell them how, Nirrao."

Nirrao, seeing that she had to give the Stony Brook wolves some instruction, seemed to recover herself. "Although you've been travelling in single file," she said, "you've been leaving a very clear trail – anyone could tell from your tracks that there were four of you here. The way we do it is to step directly into the paw-prints of the wolf in front, so that after the scent fades – you'll know that snow only holds scent for a short time – any enemy that comes upon the tracks won't know how many wolves were there."

"That explains why these tracks we found look blurred," said Kona. "Where we come from, we only travel in single file to make the going easier in the snow – there's a lot less of it there, of course. I'm afraid stepping into each other's paw-prints never occurred to us."

"I don't think it's going to work with us smaller-pawed wolves anyway," Baru commented. "We're just going to leave smaller tracks inside your larger ones."

"I'd thought of that," said Nirrao. "I'll be bringing up the rear, so that my prints mask yours. Now, follow Dargo, all of you."

They fell into line behind Dargo and set off. Soon, a forest appeared on the horizon, and they continued steadily towards it. As they drew nearer, the Stony Brook wolves saw that the trees were of a kind they had never seen before, pungent-smelling and covered with short, stiff spines, still green despite the season, instead of leaves. They grew close together, as if huddled together for warmth, their branches intertwined so that they formed a single, dark clump, like one huge tree-top with multiple trunks. It stood out in stark contrast between the snow and the pale sky.

When they reached the forest's edge, Dargo led them into it. After the dazzling brilliance of the sun on snow, the darkness beneath the trees momentarily looked absolute. They paused to allow their eyes to accustom themselves to the gloom.

Only a few chinks of light penetrated the heavy shadow cast by the trees. How dismal it seemed to the Stony Brook wolves, who were used to forests and woods where complex networks of dappled, shifting light and shade wove intricate and ever-changing patterns on the ground. How empty the spaces between the trees looked, for without light no undergrowth could grow to fill them. And how strange it was to walk not upon dry, dead leaves but upon a fallen layer of the spines that took their place. The interlaced canopy did, however, block out snow as well as light, which meant it was a little warmer here.

"What kind of trees are these?" asked Kona curiously.

"Spruce," answered Dargo, without turning. A short while later he stopped and said: "Stay here with Nirrao. I'll get Tashar."

They obligingly sat down to rest, and Dargo disappeared amongst the trees. They could tell Nirrao was almost bursting with eagerness to hear more of their story, and waited impatiently for the arrival of her leader. To pass the time, she began explaining to the newcomers why Dargo spoke so seldom and sparingly. "Several seasons ago," she said, "Dargo was injured on the hunt. He was kicked in the face by a moose – a glancing blow, thank the Alphas, else he wouldn't be here today. As it was, the kick broke his jaw."

For most creatures, a broken jaw would have meant a lingering death by starvation. Wolves, with the pack to help and care for them, are more fortunate. The others had provided for Dargo, but his injury made it impossible for him to feed in the normal way, by tearing chunks of meat from the carcass. After his first attempt failed, leaving him both hungry and in a great deal of pain, they started regurgitating partly-digested food for him, which he was able to swallow without too much difficulty. The break in his jaw eventually healed, but the bones did not join together exactly as before, and he was left with a slight speech impediment that made him reluctant to speak more than was strictly necessary.

Just as Nirrao reached the end of her tale, Dargo returned. The wolf he brought with him matched him, Nirrao and Kona in the thickness of his coat and in the size of his paws. The Stony Brook wolves had expected this, for it was the norm here in the cold land. What surprised them was that he had only one eye. The other, his left, had apparently been lost in a fight of some kind, for the sealed lids were surrounded by scar tissue. Yet his single eye held them in a gaze that was unnerving in its peculiar directness, a gaze that seemed somehow familiar. It was Jareth who saw it first.

"Kona!" she exclaimed. "Kona, it's your gaze!"

And then, as the wolf came forward to meet them, they saw that his gait, too, was Kona's, the way he moved, placed his paws, carried his tail.

"Greetings," he said, his attention fixed on Kona. "Who are you that knows the name of Rishala?"

"I am Kona," said Kona, boldly, "and Rishala was my mother."

The three wolves gasped, Nirrao and Dargo gaping at each other in disbelief. The one-eyed wolf looked long at Kona, running his disconcerting gaze over him, assessing, scrutinizing. Then his head bowed and a sigh escaped his lips.

"I am Tashar," he said solemnly, "and I am your father."

19
A New Pack

Kona and Tashar stared at each other in silence. There was so much to tell, to ask, to learn – but where to begin? Kona had imagined this moment many times during the journey from Stony Brook, and had never been able to decide what he would say.

"What happened to her?" said Tashar at length.

Kona said nothing, struggling to arrange his jumbled thoughts into some kind of order. He took a single, deep breath, as though readying himself for the coming ordeal, and then, calmly and quietly, he related to Tashar, Dargo and Nirrao the tale Garrin had told him of his birth and adoption into the Stony Brook pack. He went on to describe the turmoil he had felt upon hearing this tale himself, his decision to leave the valley and seek out the land beyond the mountains, and most of what had happened on the journey he and the others had made. Of the fight with the Beaver Lake wolves he spoke, and of the friendliness of those at Grassy Hollow. Of the killing of the moose, the meeting with Neeko, the encounter with the human and the fording of the river. Of the whispering wolves, the demise of the puma, the crossing of the mountains. The only thing he did not mention was the discovery of the bones in the wood where he had been born.

As his tale drew to a close, neither he nor his audience noticed a shape rise from the shadows downwind of them as the wolf who had been trailing Nirrao and Dargo when they first met the strangers, who had followed them back to the forest and hidden nearby, and who had seen and heard all that passed between Tashar and Kona and the others, crept away.

"I can hardly believe it," murmured Tashar. "My poor Rishala ... such a journey in her condition ..."

"Can you tell us how all this began?" asked Kona gently. "This rival pack she spoke of, how they drove her to leave?"

"Yes," said Tashar, shaking himself out of his reverie. "Yes, you have a right to know. The rival wolves are known as the Ice Creek pack – they take their name from a creek in their territory that remains ice-cold even in summer – and all this actually began a long time before they drove Rishala to leave, when they were not rivals, but friends. We respected each other's territory and lived in peace with each other, and their leader, Brogan, and I would often meet and go exploring together in the mountains. We always wondered what lay beyond, you see. But one day, while we were exploring, there was a landslide. Brogan, may the Alphas rest his soul, was killed, crushed beneath a boulder ten times the size of a wolf. His successor was his son, Ragmarr. He never quite came to terms with his father's death – he blamed me for it, and ever since has been trying to drive us out, to claim our territory for his own."

"To this day?" said Kona.

"Yes. Every so often he leads his pack in an attack against us."

"How big is his pack?" Baru wanted to know.

"There are six of them," said Tashar.

"And your numbers are ...?"

"As you see," Tashar replied. "Three."

The Stony Brook wolves were impressed that so small a pack had managed to hold its own for so long against odds of two to one, and understood why Nirrao and Dargo had not seemed daunted at being outnumbered upon meeting them.

"Please go on," Kona encouraged Tashar.

"Ragmarr launched his most determined attack when he learned Rishala was with cub," said Tashar bitterly. "He wanted no offspring of mine encroaching on his space. It was in the battle that ensued that I lost my left eye, though I also gave him a wound he won't forget. I told Rishala to run, to protect the cubs, and she fled into the mountains with two of Ragmarr's wolves in pursuit. I ... I never saw her again ... I ..."

He broke off in distress, and Dargo put in: "We searched for days. Couldn't find her."

"We never dreamed she would cross right over the mountains," continued Nirrao, "but after a time we knew she was dead. Nothing else would have kept her from Tashar."

"I'm sorry," said Kona, feeling responsible for the pain he saw on the faces of the three wolves – his father, his uncle, his aunt. "I didn't mean to re-open old wounds. Would it have been better if I'd never come?"

"No," said Tashar at once, "no, I'm glad you did. You don't know what it means to me to know that something of my beloved Rishala lives on – in you, I mean. And that I have a son. A son!"

He shook his head in wonderment.

"Then ... we can stay?" asked Jareth timidly.

"Of course you can stay! You may join my pack for as long as you wish. And now, you must be hungry. Come, we have a kill nearby."

The Stony Brook wolves soon settled in to life as part of Tashar's pack. Though there were moose in the cold land, the other hoofed animals they had been accustomed to hunting, such as elk and white-tailed and mule deer, were absent. Here the most common prey was a kind of deer called caribou, which they had never seen before. It had wide, splayed hooves for walking on the snow, and tall, elaborate antlers which, unlike any other deer species, were possessed by females as well as males. Indeed, it was currently only the females that bore them, for the males had shed theirs in late autumn, but, the Stony Brook wolves were told, at their full growth they were bigger and more extravagant than the females'. Learning the ways of these creatures and the best methods of hunting them occupied the newcomers for some time.

Shimook, Baru and Jareth adapted well, though they disliked the cold. However, as the time went by, Kona grew strangely morose and introverted, often wandering off by himself just as he had done back in Stony Brook. Baru thought his behaviour was due to resentment of surrendering his new-found leadership to Tashar, though his sisters disagreed. Nirrao and Dargo assumed he was discovering the land of his forefathers at his own pace, seeing it for himself without the distraction of his companions. Only Tashar guessed at the real reason for Kona's discomfort, suspecting that he simply did not know what to do with himself now that he had reached his journey's end.

This, indeed, was true. Kona did feel that his quest was over – he had found Rishala's land and met with her mate, his father, and been told the things he wished to know. He *did* wonder what to do next. But there was more. He had expected to begin to feel at home in the cold land after the first few days, and to feel content within himself now that he knew his origins fully. This had not happened. He felt out of place, as though he didn't belong. He was still a newcomer, and somehow he sensed that, however long he spent there, the cold land would never feel like home. And he still felt there was something missing from his life.

Throughout the journey – ever since the telling of Garrin's tale, in fact – he had been certain that it was his real family, or at least his knowledge of them, that had been missing. Now he realized it was not that simple, and even began to wonder which was his *real* real family after all. Though he had, naturally, grown very fond of Tashar, Dargo and Nirrao (and they of him), he found himself thinking with a pang of the wolves he had left behind in Stony Brook, the wolves who had raised him and loved him as their own. They knew him, and he them, in a way these new wolves, who were his blood relatives, never could. Was he wrong to have left them? No, he told himself, for if he had stayed he would never have found the answers to the questions his birth had raised, the answers which Tashar had given him. He would not have been happy.

"Yet I'm not happy now," he thought miserably. "The void in my heart is as empty as ever."

20
Kalani

One night, unable to sleep, Kona lay turning his thoughts over in his mind when the sensation of being watched came over him. He glanced sideways at Baru, the nearest wolf to him, to see if he was awake. Baru, however, was sound asleep, twitching and growling in repose as he chased some adversary along the pathways of his dreams.

Carefully, moving only his eyes, Kona scanned the area within his range of vision. He saw nothing, but the feeling of somebody's gaze on him did not diminish. He inhaled quietly through his nose. There it was! The scent of a female wolf, a stranger, somewhere behind him. He made a show of yawning and stretching, as though he had just that moment awoken, and got to his paws. Then, as if by chance taking that direction, he turned and padded towards the scent.

It led him towards a tree whose lowest branches almost swept the ground, and it was beneath these, in deep shadow, that the wolf was crouched. She looked taken aback at being discovered, her expression so like that of a naughty cub caught in some act of disobedience by a parent that he almost laughed.

"Why were you watching us?" he asked in a not unfriendly manner.

"I ... I ... I'm sorry," she stammered. "I meant no harm. I just wanted to see this wolf, this Kona they're saying is Tashar's son."

"What?" said Kona, startled. "Who's saying that?"

She peered anxiously past him at his sleeping companions before replying: "If we're going to talk, could we move a little further away? If your pack wake up and find me here ..."

She trailed off as Kona looked from her to the others and back again. He had just realized that she must be one of the Ice Creek pack and, as such, was on enemy territory and likely to be attacked if found there. She must have had considerable courage, and curiosity, to have risked coming here alone. That was assuming she *was* alone – it suddenly occurred to him that perhaps the rest of her pack was nearby, and he ought to be raising the alarm. He sniffed the air, searching for other unfamiliar wolf scents, but found none. The female certainly acted as though she was by herself – she would likely have been more confident if her pack-mates were around – but it was probably safest not to simply trust her word. He would go with her, he decided, but remain close enough to the pack that he could alert them at the first sign of trouble.

"Come on, then," he said, and together they crept further into the forest. Kona made sure that the distance between themselves and the rest of the pack was enough that they would not be woken by ordinary speech, but not so much that they wouldn't hear him if he called. Once away from their immediate vicinity, the female began to relax somewhat, and Kona asked again who had told her who he was.

"Tharg, my nephew, saw you and those others from beyond the mountains meet with the Great Peaks pack," she explained. "Is it true? That you're Tashar's son, I mean? It must be you, the other new wolves look too different."

"Yes, it's true," answered Kona. "I'm Kona and I'm Tashar's son. But you haven't told me who *you* are. I take it you're from Ragmarr's pack?"

"I am," she confirmed, looking at the ground as though ashamed of the fact. "I'm Kalani. Ragmarr is my brother."

"Your brother?" said Kona, suddenly suspicious.

"Yes, but I'm not here to spy on you for him," Kalani hastened to reassure him. "As I said, I just wanted to see this wolf, this ... you."

"And now that you have, what will you do?"

"I'll go back to my territory and go to sleep."

"You won't tell your brother you were here?"

"No!" she said emphatically. "He'd be furious if he knew. He already doubts my loyalty to the pack because I've tried to persuade him to stop this senseless feud with Tashar."

"You have?" said Kona in surprise.

"Yes. I don't want my pack and yours to be enemies just because of his absurd belief that our father's death was Tashar's fault."

"You don't believe it was?" said Kona, intrigued to learn that at least one member of the Ice Creek pack was not against the Great Peaks wolves.

"No, of course not. Tashar told us what happened – there was nothing he could have done. But Ragmarr was determined to blame him."

"What do the rest of the pack think?"

"They know it was an accident," said Kalani. "They don't follow Ragmarr against you because of my father's death – that's his own reason. He's convinced them we should drive you out because we need the territory, even though we don't. But he can't fool me. I know him too well."

"Tell me about your pack," Kona said.

"There's six of us altogether," said Kalani, "as I expect you've heard. Besides myself and Ragmarr, and his son Tharg whom I mentioned earlier, there's Chanku, my brother's mate, their daughter Luri, and my uncle, Marnov – he's black, so you'll know him if you see him. Of us all, I'm the only one who wants peace between our packs. I've tried to make them see that there's plenty of space and plenty of prey for both packs, but it's no use. I'm the omega wolf, and Ragmarr is a very assertive leader – they won't listen to me. I don't think they understand my point of view. You can't imagine how lonely it is, Kona, having no-one who understands how you feel."

"Can't I?" Kona said softly.

"*Can* you?" said Kalani, interested.

"Yes," said Kona simply, "I can."

"Really? Then do you want ... I mean, would you ... would you like to talk about it?" Kalani asked shyly. "I've always wanted someone to talk to about these things."

"Have you?" asked Kona, smiling with increasing pleasure at his new acquaintance. "So have I!"

Kalani smiled back, saying: "Then perhaps we, whom no-one else seems to understand, can understand each other."

"Perhaps we can," agreed Kona. "Where do I start? I've always felt lonely, you see – at least, as long as I can remember. I knew I was different from the rest of the pack."

"I did, too. I felt as though ... as though I was only half a wolf. As though ..."

"You weren't quite whole?" Kona finished for her. "I felt the same. And I tried to talk to them about it, but of course they didn't understand. I know I couldn't have expected them to, when I didn't really understand myself, but ... but ..."

"But you longed for someone to say: 'Oh yes, I know how you feel.'"

"Yes," said Kona quietly. "I wanted that desperately."

"So did I."

The two wolves looked at each other with a mixture of delight, sympathy and respect.

"He knows!" Kalani was saying to herself. "He knows what it's like!"

"She understands!" Kona was thinking. "She truly understands!"

And even as he started to tell her of the sense he had always had that there was something missing from his life, somewhere in his heart the conviction was beginning to grow that whatever it was, was missing no more.

They talked long into the night, often completing each other's sentences as they compared similar experiences, the memories seeming so much less painful for having been shared and understood. It was only when the impending dawn announced itself with a line of faint light along the horizon that their voices died away, and a companionable silence fell between them.

Kona felt as if he had known Kalani forever. He had bared his soul to her and she had looked upon it with compassion, for it was a reflection of her own. She knew how he felt, for she felt the same herself. She surely knew him better than any other wolf. And for the first time since he was a cub, he felt ... content.

21
The Attack

After that, Kona and Kalani met each night in the no-wolf's-land between their packs' territories. Night after night they ran together, romping and gambolling like a pair of carefree cubs with the snow flying up around them in a scintillating cloud. Until at last, tired of their play, they would lie down side by side in a sheltered spot, his fur mingling warmly with hers, and tell each other the things they could tell no-one else. And so their affinity grew and deepened, becoming a close and intimate friendship which, thanks to their mutual trust and affection, rapidly evolved into love.

Kona had never been so happy. For the first time in his life he felt complete, as though he had found a lost part of himself. The void within him was full to overflowing with love given and love received. He took delight in everything around him, glorying in the rigours of the cold land and throwing himself into the hunt with an energy that seemed to know no fatigue. Sometimes he felt ready to burst with joy, and at such times gave vent to the feeling the only way he knew how – by flinging up his head and howling out his happiness to the world.

In the beginning, he kept his meetings with Kalani secret from the pack, and she naturally had no intention of telling her brother about them. To avoid returning to their packs bearing each other's scent, they would find something pungent to roll in after separating – fallen spruce-spines, perhaps, or a carcass, or some animal dung – and then cleanse themselves by rolling in the snow or immersing themselves in water. But the change in Kona could hardly have gone unnoticed by the other Great Peaks wolves. At first they were simply glad that he had recovered from his morose and introspective mood, but when at length he confessed the reason to them, Tashar, Dargo and Nirrao were most dubious about him becoming involved with a member of the Ice Creek pack. She would betray them to her brother, they said.

"She'd never do such a thing," said Kona hotly. "You don't know her like I do – she hates this feud as much as we do. She's doing what she can to make her pack see how pointless it is. Perhaps, between us, we can establish a peace."

"And if you can't?" said Tashar. "If she has to choose between you and her brother? Her loyalty is bound to lie with her pack, you know."

Kona almost retorted that if he had to choose between Kalani and his pack he would choose her without hesitation, but he could not quite bring himself to say it. For wolves, loyalty is second nature, and although he knew Kalani loved him he began to wonder what they *would* do if they could not bring peace to their packs.

He thought of Kalani as his mate, but they had not performed the Union Song – for one thing, they could not risk Ragmarr hearing them do so, and for another, they were not pack leaders. In order for them to truly be mated, and breed when the season came, they would have to become the alpha pair of a pack, and this obviously presented difficulties. There was no chance of Kona joining Ragmarr's pack and the two of them taking over as its leaders, but would Tashar and the others accept Kalani into their pack? And if so, would Tashar be willing to step down as leader and let Kona take his place? If not, Kona supposed, then the only option would be for him to leave his pack, and Kalani hers, and the two of them start a new pack of their own.

Kalani had to be much more careful to keep her feelings concealed from her pack than Kona did. She knew Ragmarr would react with far more than disapproval if he discovered she was consorting with what he would consider a rival wolf. But she could not stop the pack noticing her frequent absences, and wondering, and soon Ragmarr announced that they would shortly make another attempt at driving out the Great Peaks pack.

"Tashar's pack is larger now," he said, "and more wolves need more food and more territory, and the less there will be for us. We must make a more determined effort to get rid of them – especially since one of these new ones is Tashar's son. I will not have his bloodline continued on land that should be ours."

Kalani, as usual, protested to the attack, though she tried to make sure she showed no more emotion about it than she had on previous occasions. She did not want Ragmarr's suspicions aroused, and besides, she knew he would go ahead with the attack whatever she said. But she could at least warn the Great Peaks wolves, through Kona, that it was coming, which she did that night at their rendezvous.

"Do you know when?" he asked.

"Not exactly," she replied, "but it'll be soon. Be ready."

"Will you be there?" said Kona.

"Oh yes. Ragmarr makes us all go, though he knows I will not strike a blow except in self-defence."

"He makes you all go?" said Kona. "But surely his mate is pregnant, now that the breeding season's come and gone. Would he risk the safety of his unborn cubs?"

"No," said Kalani, sadly. "Ragmarr and Chanku mated, of course, but she hasn't become pregnant. I blame this feud for that – it's common knowledge that stress makes it harder for a wolf to conceive."

"I'm sorry," said Kona. "There'll be no cubs in my pack, either, come the spring – my father never took another mate after my mother's death. Now, when this attack comes, shall I ask my pack to leave you be?"

"No, if they ignore me my brother will wonder why," said Kalani. "He must keep thinking your pack sees me as a foe."

"I suppose so," Kona conceded, "but I won't have you hurt. I'll pretend to attack you myself."

"That's all very well," said Kalani, "if you're not too involved in the real fighting. Ragmarr is keen to do battle with Tashar's son, and he may come straight for you. He's a fierce fighter – he's never been beaten in single combat – so you'll need to concentrate if he does."

"Well, then one of my pack will stand in for me," said Kona firmly. "But you say Ragmarr's never been beaten in single combat? Has he beaten my father, then?"

"Not exactly – they always fight pack-to-pack. Ragmarr knows there would be no point in challenging Tashar to single combat, because even if he won – which he probably would – your father would still refuse to leave his home. My brother hopes to wear him down with these constant attacks, so that in the end he'll just leave because he can't stand it any longer. Myself, I don't think that's ever going to happen."

"Neither do I," said Kona, under his breath.

Ragmarr launched his attack two days later, in the dead of night. He had expected to catch the Great Peaks pack sleeping, but to his surprise and annoyance Dargo was awake and evidently on guard.

The moment he became aware of the Ice Creek wolves' approach, he barked an alert to wake the others. Each of them had been prepared for this and were instantly up and facing their attackers.

Kona only just had time to indicate Kalani to Jareth, who had volunteered to mock-fight her, before he was confronted by Ragmarr. That it *was* Ragmarr he had no doubt, for the wolf carried himself with the assurance of one who is undisputed leader and is always obeyed. He approached with his head and tail held up, looking down his muzzle at Kona, arrogance advertising itself in every line of his body. His ears were little more than shapeless shreds, having been thoroughly ripped to pieces some time in the past. It gave him a rough, intimidating air.

"So," he growled, his voice laden with menace, "you are the son of Tashar."

"I am," said Kona, with far more composure than he felt. "And you are Ragmarr, my father's enemy."

"Your father," said Ragmarr, his lips drawing slightly back from his teeth in the prelude to a snarl, "is responsible for the death of mine. And for *this*."

He tilted the tattered remnants of his ears forward as he spoke this last.

"You are responsible for robbing my father of his left eye," Kona responded, "and for my mother's death."

The words were barely out of his mouth before Ragmarr lunged forward, his jaws agape. Kona leapt sideways, but instead of plunging past him Ragmarr swung round after him, his teeth tearing through the fur and flesh of Kona's right shoulder. He tried to strike in return, but Ragmarr had retreated out of range. Now that was strange, thought Kona, wincing. Usually it was he who could dodge other wolves, not they who could dodge him.

And then he noticed the way the wolves of the cold land fought. They were not coming to grips and fighting locked together like those on the other side of the mountains, but were avoiding contact, evading each other's charges and darting in when they saw an opening in their adversary's defences. They fought just like him! Perhaps he should have expected that, but he realized at once that it meant his method of fighting gave him no advantage here, as it had in his play-fights as a cub and his battle with Matsu. Here, it would be his adoptive siblings' manner of fighting that was unusual.

Ragmarr struck him again, slashing a wound down his neck and tangling his front legs with Kona's, tripping him up. He fell on his side, and Ragmarr's open jaws descended towards his face. Kona kicked out with his front paws, hitting Ragmarr squarely in the chest and knocking him back. Then, suddenly, Tashar was there, furiously attacking his enemy and driving him from his fallen son.

Kona sprang up and went to help him. Even to a seasoned fighter like Ragmarr, the sight of father and son advancing on him shoulder to shoulder was a formidable one. He backed away, looking round to see how the rest of his pack were faring. Kalani and one of the females from beyond the mountains were circling each other, snarling and snapping. Chanku was fighting well enough against Nirrao, and Tharg against Dargo, but Luri and Marnov appeared to be in difficulties. They were fighting the other female and the male from beyond the mountains, both of whom fought strangely – they had fastened their teeth into Luri and Marnov respectively, and were hanging on whilst trying to push their opponents to the ground. Both his own wolves were somewhat at a loss, struggling and thrashing about to no apparent effect.

"Enough!" he bellowed. The word was a command to his well-disciplined pack, and with the exception of Luri and Marnov, who were unable to do so, each of them broke at once from the fighting and assembled behind him. Unsure of what was to happen next, Shimook and Baru, still keeping a firm hold on their captives, looked to Tashar.

"Let them go," he said.

Shimook and Baru complied, and Ragmarr's daughter and uncle ran to join their companions. Then the Ice Creek pack turned and made off into the night, Ragmarr in the lead and the others strung out behind him. Last to leave, and with many a backward glance, was Kalani.

22
'All Good Things Must Come to an End'

Spring came late to the cold land, but come it did, eventually. The weather warmed and the snow melted, except for in the higher reaches of the mountains, and the moose and caribou gave birth, making it a time of plenty for the wolves, for the calves, inexperienced as they were, made easy prey. Despite this, the season felt rather cheerless to Kona. He had noticed an unwelcome change coming over Kalani ever since the battle between their packs – she seemed preoccupied, as though there was something constantly on her mind, and was less inclined to frolic with him than she had been before Ragmarr's attack. He guessed she was feeling the strain of keeping their meetings secret from her brother, and of being torn by conflicting loyalties. But when he asked her about it, she said: "It isn't that. Nothing's wrong, really. I've just been doing a lot of thinking. I'd rather not talk about it."

"You can talk to me, surely?" said Kona, rather upset by her sudden reluctance to share her thoughts with him. "You can tell me anything, Kalani, you know that. Whatever it is that's bothering you, I'll be here for you. You can rely on me."

As touching as his concern for her was, rather than consoling her it only appeared to trouble her more. For the first time since they met, Kona did not feel at one with her. He grew frustrated and irritable – first with Kalani, for her unwillingness to talk, and then with himself, for his inability (as it seemed to him) to give her the understanding she needed. Doubt and anxiety gnawed at him as he became more and more desperate to know what the matter was, and, as much as he loved her, he began to resent Kalani for not telling him.

And then, one night, she did not arrive to meet him in the appointed place. Kona was worried, but not unduly so – on certain previous occasions she had been forced to avoid their usual rendezvous site by members of her pack roaming further afield than they ordinarily did. She was probably waiting for him somewhere else. He searched the no-wolf's-land, checking all their favourite haunts twice over and even venturing as far as the borders of her pack's territory, but to no avail. Kalani was nowhere to be found. He wondered briefly if he should press on into Ragmarr's domain, but decided not to risk it. She must be unable to meet him for some reason, he thought – she would explain everything the next night.

But when, the following night, she again failed to arrive, Kona started to worry seriously. Again he searched for her in all likely spots, and again he found no trace. Finally he stood again at the borders of her home ground, and knew that this time he would have to enter. He was afraid, certainly, but his desire to see Kalani outweighed his fear of what might happen should the Ice Creek pack catch him trespassing. He stepped over the boundary into hostile territory.

He proceeded with the utmost caution, every sense alert, keeping to paths that were under cover. When he had no choice but to venture into open areas, he crossed them quickly and quietly, keeping low to the ground and taking care not to leave tracks. He had not gone far when he caught the scent of the pack ahead of him, and crept towards them. He stopped behind a convenient screen of undergrowth and peered through it at the wolves lying stretched out before him, their sides rising and falling rhythmically as they slept.

His gaze settled on Kalani, who was a short distance away from the others in the shadow of a tree. He could not see her face, and it was only when she sighed and rolled over that he realized she was awake. Now, as she lay with her head on her front paws, she was turned slightly in his direction and the moonlight picked out her expression. It was one of such sadness that Kona wanted to run to her and comfort her, though he could not imagine why she should be so sad.

"Kalani!" he called softly. "Kalani!"

Kalani's head jerked up at the sound of her name, and she looked this way and that for a moment, before some slight movement of Kona's betrayed his hiding place. Seeing him, her face hardened and she strode across to him angrily.

"What are you doing here?" she demanded, almost growling. "Don't you know the danger you're in?"

"Yes, of course," he replied, "but I wanted to see you. Where have you been, Kalani? Why haven't you come to meet me these last two nights?"

"Because I didn't want to!" Kalani snapped.

"Wha ... what?" faltered Kona, bewildered.

"I didn't want to," Kalani repeated. "I belong with my pack, and you with yours. We're rivals, you and I. Enemies, even."

"But you don't believe that!" exclaimed Kona, scarcely able to believe his ears. "We make each other happy – we shouldn't let our packs interfere with that."

"I admit I enjoyed your company at first," said Kalani, "but all good things must come to an end."

A cold dread clutched at Kona's heart as the horrible truth of what was happening suddenly dawned on him. Could she really mean what he thought she meant? "What are you saying, Kalani?" he asked her.

"I'm saying I don't love you any more, Kona. In fact, I don't think I ever did. It was just the excitement of meeting someone new, of defying my brother."

All Kona's strength seemed to drain out of him at these words. His legs trembled and he collapsed. He struggled to say something, anything, but found himself unable to speak – his chest felt tight and constricted, and he could hardly breathe. He lay there, gasping, staring pleadingly up at the wolf he loved, mutely imploring her to take back what she had said. She looked away, and said more gently: "I'm sorry, Kona. I never meant to hurt you. Go now, and don't ever come here again. You'll regret it if you do."

Then she turned her back and walked away. Kona watched her go, his mind reeling, his heart breaking, until she disappeared into a stand of trees. Almost as soon as she was gone, a kind of disbelieving daze descended on him. Numb with shock, he could not bring himself to believe that Kalani did not love him, so awful was the idea, and consequently he blanked out much of what had just happened. For a long time he did not move, but eventually, not bothering to conceal himself or his tracks, he dragged himself to his paws and made his way back to his own territory.

There, still unable to think clearly, he wandered aimlessly here and there, and had climbed some distance into the mountains before he realized where he was. It was then that the events of the night came flooding back to him, sweeping through the daze in a great wave of grief and anguish. Kalani had told him she did not love him, and with that recollection came the knowledge that he would never run or play or talk with her again.

That moment was perhaps the worst in all Kona's life. It was as though the world had suddenly crumbled around him, leaving him floating in infinite nothingness, the last living creature in existence. Never, never had he felt so alone. The feeling welled up inside him, growing and expanding until he could contain it no longer. Then, standing on a rocky outcrop, an isolated silhouette against the waning moon, Kona threw back his head and howled out his woe. Out into the uncaring vastness of the sky went his Heart Song; forlorn, plaintive and profoundly mournful. A song, like all wolf songs, that had no words, but was instead the unmitigated sound of raw emotion. A song of pure sorrow.

To the wolves who woke to it in the land below, it was as though loneliness itself was giving voice.

23
Misery

The pack found him the next morning in a cave on the lower slopes of the mountain, curled up in the darkness at its back and whining pitifully to himself in his distress. He told them, as briefly as he could, what had happened, and then turned from them and would say no more.

The days that followed were agony for Kona, an emotional agony far worse than any physical pain he had ever experienced. The void he had had in his heart before meeting Kalani, and which her love had filled, was nothing to the one her loss left behind. It was a bottomless chasm inside him; an empty, endless ache. His misery grew until it was overwhelming, infiltrating every aspect of his being, becoming all that he felt, all that he thought, all that he was. He remembered the tale of how wolves came to be, of how, because Alpha-she had been created from part of Alpha-he's soul, the souls of all mated pairs after them became one. It truly seemed to Kona that, without Kalani, he was incomplete – that half his soul was missing. Losing her was like losing a part of himself. Sometimes he cursed Alpha-he for accepting such grief for his descendents when he asked the Great Spirit for a mate.

Try as they might during this time, the other wolves could not persuade Kona to leave the cave. He refused to emerge even to hunt, and they brought him a share of each kill, in their mouths if they killed nearby or in their stomachs if the carcass was further away. However, he ate less and less as the days passed. Despair was gnawing away at him, sapping his will to live. There did not seem much point in feeding, in keeping himself alive and in such anguish.

The pack came to visit him daily, letting him know they cared. At first they tried to convince him that there were still things to enjoy and look forward to, but soon gave up when he responded by saying absolutely nothing. After a while, they took to lying silently beside him, licking him sympathetically and trying simply to comfort him with their presence. Once, Baru attempted to dispel Kona's gloom by reminding him of greater challenges (as he saw them) he had overcome.

"Think of everything you did on our journey here, Kona," he urged him. "Remember how you defeated Matsu and got us safely away from his pack? And how you overcame your fear of the human, and looked upon it without running away, even when it made that dreadful noise? Then there's the puma – you drew it off when it was coming to kill me. You risked your own life to save mine."

"I shall throw myself into the jaws of the next puma I see," growled Kona sullenly, without looking up. This so upset Baru that he could not face visiting Kona for several days afterwards.

Another time, the visitors came bearing the marks of the teeth of Ragmarr's wolves, having again been attacked by the Ice Creek pack. If Kona noticed, he did not say so, and they too refrained from mentioning it. Instead, they tried to cajole him into talking about what he was going through, thinking it might help him to share his feelings. All he said to this was: "You wouldn't understand."

"But," said Nirrao to Tashar later, "you and I and Dargo do understand how it feels to lose someone you love. We lost Rishala, didn't we?"

"You and Dargo lost a sister and a friend," Tashar replied. "That's a different kind of love, and so a different kind of loss. But as to me – you may have something there, Nirrao. For me the loss of Rishala was a similar experience to his. Perhaps, knowing that I suffered as he does, he'll be willing to speak to me if I go and see him alone."

He went the next day, and, standing over his son where he lay facing the back of the cave, told him gently: "You have to be brave, Kona. I know at the moment you feel as though you can't go on, but time is a great healer. Don't give up yet. One day life will seem worth living again."

Kona rolled over and looked up at him out of eyes full of torment, their brightness dimmed by the shadow of his sadness.

"It hurts so much," he said, his voice low and devoid of all hope, "so very much. I can't believe it will ever stop hurting."

This was the first time he had spoken of how he was feeling. Encouraged, Tashar continued. "I know, my son, I know. The heart can hurt more than the deepest wound. Perhaps the pain won't ever go away completely, but it does diminish with time, so that you can control it, rather than having it control you. I felt the same as you do when I lost Rishala – it hurt me so badly that I wanted to die. I will always miss her, of course, but now I can bear the pain ..."

"She loved you," Kona interrupted. "You lost her because she died, not because she didn't want you."

"I still lost her."

"It's not the same," insisted Kona, "it's not the same."

"It's the same principle. What I'm trying to say is that if you can just find the courage to endure the pain, it will eventually subside. Believe me, Kona. I know this for truth."

He departed then, leaving Kona to think about what he had said. Kona did think about it, even acknowledged that in Tashar's case it might well be true, but he was sure that such pain as his own could never subside.

A couple of days later, his adoptive siblings came to the cave saying they had something important to discuss with him. He said listlessly: "Nothing's important to me any more, except *her*. The only thing I care about is a wolf who doesn't care about me."

"Just listen," said Baru. Kona waited, and after a pause Jareth said: "We want to go home, Kona."

"Home?" said Kona, puzzled. "This is our home."

"This place can never be a real home to us," Jareth told him. "It's too cold here, too bleak and harsh."

"Don't you see, Kona?" said Shimook. "We came here for you. We stayed because you stayed. We follow Tashar because you do, and you are our leader."

"And you don't really feel at home here either, do you?" said Baru. "You might have left once you'd met your father and learned more of your mother, if it wasn't for Kalani. So now you no longer have a reason to remain here, we want you to lead us back to our real home. Back to Stony Brook."

"Stony Brook?" said Kona in surprise. "But ... but I can't. I can't just leave Kalani's homeland, the place I met her, the place we were so happy. I can't."

"Will you ever forget Kalani?" Shimook asked him.

"No!" said Kona vehemently. "I'll never forget her as long as I live!"

"Then you'll remember her and what you had together however far you are from the place it happened," said Shimook. "You can remember her just as well in Stony Brook as you can here."

Kona stared at her. She was probably right, but he still did not think he could face the prospect of leaving. He said so, and Shimook answered: "It's up to you, of course, Kona. We won't go without you. But we want to return to Stony Brook, and we want you to lead us there. Please think about it."

Soon after this, Tashar came once more to visit Kona by himself, and after telling him again that he would feel better in time, he asked him if he had considered his adoptive siblings' request.

"Yes, I've considered it," Kona replied, "but I don't think I could stand to be that far away from Kalani. And there's you, too – you and Dargo and Nirrao. I'd miss you all very much."

"And we would miss you, but we'd always have our memories to remind us of each other. We want what's best for you, Kona, and we think you'd be happier in Stony Brook. I know it'll be hard for you to leave, but your pack needs you to lead them from here. Be brave, Kona, for their sakes if not for your own."

Kona's face took on a far-away expression as Tashar spoke these words, for he was remembering a time – not so long ago, and yet it felt like a life-time – when another wolf had spoken to him of leadership and bravery. He had said: "It will be your duty to them to see that your own feelings do not interfere with the needs of the pack. There will be times when this will be difficult for you – every leader faces such times. Remember then what I told you of courage."

And he whispered to himself: "Courage does not mean having no fear. It means *conquering* your fear."

24
Departure

A few days later, Dargo returned from taking Kona his share of their latest kill with the meat still in his mouth. He dropped it in front of him and stood looking meaningfully round at the rest of the pack. They looked back at him expectantly, awaiting an explanation. When none was forthcoming, Nirrao prompted him: "Why have you brought the meat back? Where's Kona?"

"Gone," said Dargo, with characteristic brevity.

"What do you mean, gone?" cried Jareth. "He's not in the cave?"

"Not in the cave," Dargo confirmed. The wolves stared at each other, unsure whether this was good news or bad. It had been spring when Kona had gone into retreat. Three times the moon had risen full over the mountains since then, and it was now high summer (though one considerably cooler than the Stony Brook wolves were accustomed to). And now, suddenly, he had emerged. Why?

"Did you try to track him?" asked Baru.

"No trail," said Dargo. "Rain this morning."

"Well, we must find him," said Shimook, moving off.

"We'll howl to him first," said Tashar, halting her. "Then, if he doesn't respond, we'll split up and search for him."

So saying, the six wolves lifted their voices in Contact Song. They were totally unprepared for the response they received. Kona's howl rang out clearly from somewhere close by and, though it still held an undertone of sadness, it was filled with a new note of purpose and – dare they believe it? – hope.

***

Garrin's words had echoed in Kona's head long after he had first been reminded of them. He had a duty to his pack – he knew that now. He was their leader, and it was his responsibility to do what was best for them, in spite of his own feelings. But could he bring himself to do it? While he remained here in the cold land, he could at least hear Kalani's howls and catch her scent – maybe even see her from time to time, if her pack persisted in attacking the Great Peaks wolves, or if he himself risked entering her territory for the sake of a brief glimpse of her while she slept. Could he bear to be so far from her that he would never, ever see her again?

As he thought about it he found, to his astonishment, that the pain of his yearning for her was somehow less severe than it had been. It still gripped him, because he still loved her, but it was no longer a constant torment tearing at his heart. It had become a low, dull ache somewhere deep inside him – a persistent ache, to be sure, but one he could suppress and almost ignore.

With this discovery came the possibility that, perhaps, he could leave the cold land. It hurt him to be near Kalani and yet unable to touch her or even speak to her – the hurt tainted all his memories of their time together. As Shimook had said, he could remember her just as well in Stony Brook as he could here, and maybe, further from her, he could remember the happiness they had shared without the hurt getting in the way. It was, he decided, just a case of summoning the will-power to leave.

"I will conquer my fear of leaving," he growled to himself with determination. "I will have courage!"

***

As Kona trotted up to rejoin the pack, he was moved by their evident delight to see him out and about again. They converged on him, licking and nuzzling him as though they could scarcely believe he was really there.

"My son," murmured Tashar, "I'm so glad you have come back to us. There were times when I wondered if you would."

"My heart is broken," Kona replied, "but my spirit is not."

Tashar looked as though he understood, but the other wolves were rather mystified by this remark.

"Are you ... recovered, then?" queried Baru, a little unsure as to how to phrase his question.

"I've started to recover, I think," said Kona. "My heart is still broken, but it's started to mend – though whether it will ever mend completely I don't know."

"I'm not sure I understand," said Baru.

"Before," said Kona, attempting to explain, "it was like ... like being trapped in a long, dark tunnel with no prospect of escape. Now, though I haven't quite escaped, I can see the light at the end of the tunnel."

"If his spirit had broken along with his heart," Tashar elaborated, "it would have died, and when the spirit dies the body soon follows. He would have been unable to overcome his misery, and, having no will

103

or wish to survive, would have stopped eating altogether. In the end, he would just have wasted away. It's not so uncommon, when a wolf loses his or her mate. I believe it happened to Ragmarr's mother after Brogan's death. It nearly happened to me. But my spirit did not quite break, and neither has Kona's."

"I think I understand," said Shimook, and the others solemnly agreed.

"I want to thank you all for not giving up on me, even though I nearly gave up on myself," said Kona. "And now ..."

"Yes?" said Jareth eagerly.

"Now I will lead you home."

"Then when do we leave?" exclaimed Jareth jubilantly.

"Today," he answered, not looking at Tashar or Dargo or Nirrao as he spoke, "at once. This is the hardest thing I've ever had to do and ... and if I don't go now, I might never again have the courage."

"Very well," said Tashar, bowing his head. "Then the time has come to say goodbye."

"You could come with us," Kona offered lamely.

"We belong here," said Tashar, simply. "This is our home."

Again the wolves pressed close, nuzzling and licking, whispering farewells. Then Shimook, Baru and Jareth drew back, allowing Kona a moment of privacy with his kin.

"Goodbye, my family," he said. "Thank you for taking us in, for giving me the knowledge I sought of my heritage, and for supporting me when I needed it. I shall miss you terribly. It has been a privilege being part of the Great Peaks pack."

"It has been a privilege having you here," said Tashar, his voice at once warm with affection and sombre at their imminent parting. "I am proud to have sired such a brave and worthy wolf. Remember all that your suffering has taught you, and remember us. We will be thinking of you always. Goodbye, my son. May the Alphas go with you."

Dargo, as so often, said nothing, and Nirrao too was unable to speak, but their feelings were plain to be seen on their faces. For the final time, Kona nuzzled each of them, then turned resolutely away and took his place at the head of his adoptive siblings. He did not look back as they began the climb into the mountains, but after some distance was stopped by the lugubrious howling that rose up behind him – a doleful Heart Song mourning their departure.

A short while after dusk two days later, they reached the summit of the pass between the Great Peaks and stood again at the boundary between the two lands. Here, after Shimook, Baru and Jareth had passed over the divide, Kona paused for one last look over the land they had left. The horizon was a belt of dark trees, silhouettes outlined against the star-spangled backdrop of the sky, whilst the moonlight cast an eerie, spectral luminosity over the great open expanse in the foreground. Down there somewhere, thought Kona to himself, Kalani lay sleeping. He felt as though he was leaving his heart behind him.

He howled, a soft, sad howl that pierced the night and quavered on the still air. An unheard farewell to his lost love.

25
Fire and Faith

As they descended into the forest that lay below the mountains, the wolves were disturbed to find evidence of drought in Galtag's territory. The air was hot, especially in comparison to conditions in the cold land, with no hint of moisture. From want of water the leaves on the trees were withered and prematurely brown, and the undergrowth brittle and dusty. The ground felt unusually hard under their pads, and when they pawed aside the leaf litter they found beneath not moist, decaying humus, but dry, cracked soil, all the dampness leached out of it.

"I hope the pack are managing," said Shimook in consternation.

"So do I," said Kona. "I think we'd better call them with a Contact Song."

They had been intending to surprise the pack, entering their territory without announcing themselves and then tracking them down, but now they were concerned for their friends and wanted to find them as soon as possible. They howled twice before an answer came. Following the sound towards its source, they came upon the whole pack coming to greet them – and not only were they all there, all well, and all delighted to see them, but their ranks had been swelled by the addition of three half-grown cubs, obviously born that spring.

"Welcome!" said Galtag, wagging his tail enthusiastically, and they noticed that although he still spoke in a low voice, it was not quite the whisper of earlier days. They were beginning to break the habit. "I'm so pleased to see you again! But what are you doing back here? Didn't you find what you were looking for in the cold land?"

"Yes," said Kona with a rueful smile, "but not in the way I expected."

Galtag looked a little confused. "What do you mean?" he said. "Did you find your father, or not?"

"Yes, I found him, and an uncle and aunt, too. And I'm very glad I did so, but it turns out they weren't what was missing from my life, as I'd thought. What was missing was a soul-mate."

Galtag's confusion increased. He pondered Kona's words briefly before saying: "I think you're going to have to tell me all about it."

"I will," said Kona, "but first, what's been happening here?"

"Drought, as I expect you can tell," Galtag answered. "We've had no rain since early spring. You can see the plants shrivelling, and most of our drinking places have dried up."

"What are you going to do if it continues?" asked Kona.

"If it goes on for too much longer, I'm concerned we might be left without any source of water at all," replied Galtag worriedly. "In that case, we're going to have to relocate to somewhere nearer the river."

As it turned out, however, the pack would soon be forced to relocate by something far more frightening than lack of water.

It happened three days later, as the wolves, replete after a successful hunt, were resting and talking at leisure around the remains of the elk they had killed. As they exchanged news and told tales of their respective packs, they began to notice a strange, acrid scent creeping into their nostrils, a scent which, though they did not recognize it, awoke in each of them a vague feeling of unease. Breaking off their discussions, they rose and started to mill about, restless and uncertain. Then Zari, her voice rising in mounting panic, said: "Look! What's *that*?"

Turning, the others saw a weird, flickering glow between the trees, like a sunset that had fallen to earth and shattered into a million trembling, wavering parts. At the same moment the wind shifted its direction and a blast of heat rushed over them.

"Fire!" shrieked Jareth. "Run! Run for your lives!"

Though none of the wolves had experienced fire, all had been warned of the danger it represented, yet they feared it not only from what they had heard but from a deep, primal instinct. They fled away, but now the wind was fanning the flames and they roared through the dry undergrowth with horrifying rapidity. The hissing, snapping, crackling sound of burning was all around them, and clouds of smoke filled the air, making them cough and stinging their eyes.

A long tongue of flame licked hungrily around a tree directly in front of them, racing up the trunk and splitting into countless separate flames as it burst into the branches. There was a sizzling, as of boiling sap, then a groaning, splintering, tearing noise as the dying tree heaved up its roots and smashed down through its neighbours, setting them alight as it fell and thudding into the ground with a great, shuddering crash.

Now the fire was not only behind but ahead and above, spreading from tree to tree as well as from bush to bush and through the leaf litter. New flames sprouted on all sides, as though intent on encircling the terrified wolves. They kept running, for they had no other choice.

Suddenly, Kona stopped in mid-stride, one front paw raised to take a step that was never completed. He swung round, peering back through the billowing smoke as if he could see something other than the greedy flames devouring the forest. The others pulled up and returned to his side.

"What is it, Kona?" shouted Shimook.

"Didn't you hear that?" he asked.

"Hear what?" barked Baru.

"A howl," said Kona, so quietly that the others had to strain their ears to make out his words. "I ... I thought I heard a howl."

"But we're all here," said Galtag. "Who could it have been?"

Kona was silent for several moments, looking as though he knew the answer but was unsure of the reaction it would provoke. Finally, with calm certainty, he replied: "Kalani."

Then, before any of them could make a move to stop him, he was running back towards the fire.

"Kona!" Jareth screamed. "Come back!"

"I must help her!" he called back as he ran. "You keep going – don't stop for anything! We'll catch you up!"

The other wolves were left staring at the swirling patch of smoke through which Kona had vanished. They hesitated, torn between their desire to follow him and their desire to escape, before a wall of flame rose between them and the way Kona had gone, an impassable barrier preventing them from going after him.

***

Kona knew he was risking his life, and he was afraid, but love is a force far greater than reason or fear, and though his mind urged him to flee, to save himself while he still could, his heart drove him on in search of Kalani. He was aware that the others had not heard her howl, that they did not really believe he had heard it either, but he knew he had. It had been less a call for help than a cry of terror and hopelessness. What she was doing on this side of the mountains he had no idea, but she was here somewhere, trapped by the fire, and it was up to him to save her.

He howled out a Contact Song periodically as he went, thinking to go towards her response in order to find her, but no response came. Time and again the searing heat felt almost close enough to singe his fur; time and again he backed off, circled round, and pressed on. Worse than the flames was the smoke, for it was impossible to breathe without inhaling it. It made him choke and splutter, numbing his nose, parching his mouth and catching in his throat, forcing his lungs to labour harder and harder for air. He was beginning to feel light-headed when at last, by sheer luck, he stumbled upon Kalani.

She was lying on her side at the base of a tree. As he approached, he realized that she was utterly still. Alarm surged through him as he sprang across to her. There was no mark of burning on her body, but he had no way of telling how much smoke she had inhaled. The dreadful thought occurred to him that she might have suffocated. He laid a paw on her exposed side and, to his intense relief, felt it rise and fall with a shallow breath. She was alive! He nuzzled her and licked her face, repeatedly saying her name, frantically trying to wake her before he too succumbed to the effects of the smoke and slipped into unconsciousness. She did not stir.

He seized her by the scruff of her neck, half carrying and half dragging her in the direction of safety. In his desperation, he gripped harder than he had intended and his teeth nipped Kalani's skin. She gave a small yelp of pain, twitched in his jaws, and woke.

Kona released his hold, and she lay on the ground, gazing about her without seeming to see her surroundings. Then she looked up at him and, as recognition dawned, several different emotions competed for expression on her face.

"Kona?" she said, disbelieving. "Kona? Is ... is that you?"

"Yes," said Kona, "it's me. Are the rest of your pack here somewhere?"

"No ... just me. Kona ..."

"Can you get up?"

"I ... I think so. But ... but we have to talk ... I have to explain ..."

"Plenty of time for that later," said Kona. "Right now we must concentrate on getting out of here. Come on."

Kalani looked about her as though noticing the fire for the first time. She got to her paws, swaying a little, and leaned against Kona for support. Then she seemed to recover her balance, and together they set off through the blazing forest.

***

Out on the grassland beyond the forest, the other wolves had stopped when they discovered that the fire did not seem to be advancing beyond the trees. Here they waited with trepidation for the reappearance of the one wolf missing from their number.

Time passed. They paced back and forth, their anxiety growing, unwilling to move further away, unwilling to consider the possibility that Kona might not return. Then a movement caught Neeko's attention and he squinted into the fire, trying to make out what he had glimpsed against the flames. A wolf? No – there were two!

"There he is!" he cried. "And there's someone else with him!"

All eyes turned to see, and Shimook exclaimed: "It's Kalani!"

A few moments later, the two wolves had dashed in amongst them and collapsed breathlessly on the ground. The others looked on with broad smiles as Kona and Kalani, reunited, lay there side by side, panting too hard to speak.

26
Progress

Night fell soon after Kona and Kalani's return, and these two remained wakeful long after the others had fallen asleep. For a while they watched the forest burn without speaking, though each had things they wanted to say. In the end, it was Kalani who broke the silence.

"Thank you for what you did back there, Kona," she said without looking away from the fire. "You saved my life. I would have suffocated if I'd lain there much longer, or been engulfed by the flames."

"You're welcome," he replied, a little awkwardly. He too continued to watch the fire as he spoke. "What made you leave the cold land?"

"You," said Kalani. "I followed you. When I heard you were going back to Stony Brook, I realized ... I realized how foolish I'd been. I realized ..."

She trailed off. Kona waited, wanting desperately to ask another question but afraid of what the answer might be. When Kalani did not go on, he took a deep breath and said tentatively: "You realized ... you still loved me?"

"Oh, Kona," said Kalani ruefully, "I knew I loved you all along."

Kona's heart leapt, and at the same time a puzzled frown furrowed his brow. "Then why ...?" he began.

"Why did I say I didn't? To protect you, Kona – to protect you from my brother. After the way he attacked you that night, I started thinking about what he might do if he found out about us ... I couldn't stand the thought of you getting seriously hurt because of me. I thought if we stopped seeing each other, you'd be safer, and I knew you wouldn't agree to it if I just suggested it. I'm so sorry, Kona – I know now that I hurt you more than Ragmarr ever could."

Kona was stunned. Her wish to protect him had been greater than her desire to be with him! That must have taken incredible courage. He did not know if he could have voluntarily deprived himself of her company for any reason, even her own safety. He felt ashamed to admit it to himself, but it was true.

"But the thing was," Kalani went on, "I always knew I could still go and see you if I wanted to. And then I heard you'd left the Great

111

Peaks pack, and my heart ached at the thought of never seeing you again. I hadn't really considered it before, you see, and when I did I found I couldn't bear it. So I decided to go after you."

"Did you tell the pack you were leaving?"

"No, I just crept away in the night. I wasn't sure whether or not I'd be coming back. It was all down to you, Kona – if you no longer loved me when I found you, I would simply tell you how sorry I was and go home ..."

"And if I did still love you?"

"If you did," said Kalani, half nervous, half hopeful, "*if* you did, I would ask to accompany you back to Stony Brook ... as your mate."

"Oh, Kalani," cried Kona joyfully, "do you really need to ask?"

At last they turned to look at each other, each gazing into the other's eyes and seeing the love that filled them. A moment later they were nestled against one another, he tenderly licking her face, she lovingly nuzzling his neck.

"We'll never be apart again," Kona vowed quietly. "We belong to each other, you and I. We always have."

"And we always will," said Kalani.

As one, they began the howl, lifting their voices joyously in the Union Song, their declaration to the world of their pledge to one another. They were mated, bonded for life, their souls entwined for all eternity.

They slept where they were, their bodies pressed together, their hearts beating in time.

The wolves woke the next morning to find that the fire had burnt itself out during the night. Galtag's pack looked back dejectedly at what was left of their territory – the trees reduced to lumps of charred, crumbling wood, the undergrowth completely incinerated. A fine dusting of ash covered everything.

"We're homeless!" wailed Wyanath, to which her mate said comfortingly: "We still have each other."

"But where will we go, Father?" Zari wanted to know.

"I have an idea," said Neeko. "During my time as a lone wolf, I lived for a while near where I first met Kona and the others, and there was an area there that I think would make a good territory. It had plenty of prey and so forth, and no pack had laid claim to it."

"Well, we don't seem to have much choice," said Galtag pragmatically. "Kona, it appears you and your pack are to have some company for part of your journey. Lead on, Neeko."

The two packs left at once, there being no reason to linger where they were. After hearing the Union Song the night before, no-one had been in any doubt that Kalani would be joining them. Shimook, Baru and Jareth embraced her into their pack without reservation, thrilled for Kona and glad to be able to get to know his new mate. As for Galtag and his pack, they were simply pleased to have the opportunity to meet the wolf their friend had spoken of with such obvious longing and love.

Later that day, they crossed the river at almost the same point Kona and his companions had used when journeying in the opposite direction. On the other side, they found less pronounced evidence of the drought, and even this gradually dwindled in the days that followed as summer drew to a close until, as the cooler, wetter autumn weather set in, it disappeared altogether.

These were days of largely uneventful travel, though without an established territory it was difficult finding food for so many. A routine was developed in which some of the wolves, usually in pairs, would range out to either side of the main group during the course of each day, searching for prey and howling a summons if they found it. Kona and Kalani volunteered often for scouting duty, and no-one begrudged them the opportunity to renew their bond in private.

Their delight in being together again, and the depth of their feeling for each other, were touching to see. Kona's eyes shone and his step was light and springy, his happiness expressing itself in all his movements. For Kalani, who of course had never seen deciduous trees decked out in their autumnal splendour, the season was enchanting, and nothing gave her greater pleasure than to run with Kona through the falling leaves, chasing, tumbling, play-fighting, laughing. Their happiness spread to the rest of the pack, and even to Galtag's wolves, so that a mood of cheerful excitement prevailed in them all.

There was, however, a period of tension when they reached the forest where the human had slain the elk. Just entering the forest again was a strain on the nerves of those who had witnessed that dreadful event, and even those who had not experienced the terror a human inspired were cautious. It was not that they really expected it

113

to be there – indeed, they ascertained almost at once that it was not – but the place reminded them of the horror.

 Once through the forest and into the region where Kona, Shimook, Baru and Jareth had killed the moose and met with Neeko, the time came for the two packs go their separate ways. Neeko told them that the province he had thought of for their new territory lay a day or two's travel in the direction he had originally come from, and besides, none of Galtag's pack wanted to set up home near the forest.

 "Where a human's been once, it may be again," was how Galtag put it.

 They parted with affection, each pack wishing the other luck and the blessing of the Alphas before setting off. As they went, Kona noticed that Kalani glanced back several times, even once Galtag and his wolves were out of sight. At first he assumed she was just sad at their parting, as he was himself, but none of the others felt a need to look back, and after a while he began to wonder whether something else was troubling her.

27
Pursuit

"What's the matter, Kalani?"

Kalani jumped at the sound of Kona's voice. She had been standing with her back to the other wolves, who were still feeding on the mule deer they had killed, with her head lowered as she stared into the distance. She had not heard Kona approach.

"I ... I'm not sure," she answered pensively. "It's just ... you know how you can sometimes sense it when you're being watched?"

"Yes," said Kona, and smiled. "I sensed you watching me the night we met."

"Did you? Well, that's the feeling I keep getting – like someone's gaze is fixed on me. Sometimes it feels like they're right behind me, but when I turn to look there's no-one there."

"You're probably just on edge because you're in new country," said Kona soothingly. "Don't let it worry you. It's not far now to Grassy Hollow – you might feel better once you meet Valzir's pack. It'll take your mind off it."

"Perhaps," Kalani said, unconvinced.

***

When Ragmarr summoned his pack together for a hunt, he was not at first unduly concerned that Kalani did not appear. She often wandered off by herself – it had long been a habit of hers – and always returned in good time with no harm having befallen her. Lately, too, she had not been participating much in hunts and other pack activities, seeming strangely sad and withdrawn – he had questioned her about it, but received no clear answer.

It was not until a night and a day had passed with Kalani failing to return that he began to feel anxious. He may have possessed an obsessive hatred of Tashar, but he was as devoted to his own pack as any wolf – he loved his sister and was worried for her safety. He ordered his wolves to split up and search for her, telling them to howl a Contact Song if they found her or, if none of them did, to meet at dusk on the site of their most recent kill.

It was shortly after sunset when the last wolf, Marnov, arrived back at the appointed place, looking distinctly uneasy. He could not have found Kalani, thought Ragmarr, but he had evidently found something – something he was sure his leader wasn't going to like.

"What did you find?" he asked his uncle without preliminaries.

"I found her trail," Marnov replied, and stopped.

"You found her trail, but you didn't find her? Why didn't you keep following it until you caught up with her?"

"It … it led into the Great Peaks pack's territory," said Marnov, obviously uncomfortable with having to give Ragmarr the news, "and right through it, up into the mountains. I followed it far enough to know she was intending to cross over them, then I turned back."

"Cross over the mountains?" Ragmarr exclaimed. "Why would she do such a thing?"

"There's more," Marnov continued, his discomfiture growing with every moment. "You see, she was … well, she was following a trail herself. She was tracking Tashar's son and his companions."

"What? What in the world would make her …?" Ragmarr broke off as confusion gave way to sudden understanding. He remembered how, shortly after Kona had joined Tashar's pack, Kalani had started to behave erratically. She had seemed happy, yet nervous, particularly around him, and had tried harder than ever to convince the others that attacking the Great Peaks wolves was futile. And she had spent more time by herself than ever before.

"Except she wasn't by herself, was she?" he growled furiously. "She was with *him*! And now she's deserted her own pack to go chasing after the son of our enemy!"

Marnov, who had reached the same conclusion and accurately predicted Ragmarr's reaction, had retreated to where the rest of the pack were waiting and listening. Shaking with rage, their leader strode over to them.

"We will go after her," he announced, forcing himself to speak calmly, though his voice trembled with the effort of holding his anger in check. "We will find her, and we will bring her back."

The other wolves exchanged glances. None of them had ever seen Ragmarr so angry, or so irrational. True, it was something of a shock that Kalani should have followed Kona, and they would miss her, but she had chosen to leave – what was the use of going after her?

"Ragmarr, you can't make her come back," said Chanku reasonably. "And even if you did, what good would it do, if she wants to be gone?"

"She is my sister!" shouted Ragmarr. "She belongs here, with us!"

"Every wolf has the right to leave the pack and find a mate if they so wish," Chanku pointed out.

"But *him*? Our enemy's son? No! I cannot allow it!"

"It's not your choice, Ragmarr, it's hers. I admit it might have been awkward if he was still living here, in our land, but he isn't. He's gone. He's not our problem any more."

"We are going after her," Ragmarr stated flatly. "That's final. Even if she does want him as a mate, he can't have wanted her, or he'd have taken her with him. In which case, following him is just putting herself in danger for no reason, and it's our duty to find her and bring her safely home. We can explain that to her if we catch her before she catches him, make her see she's made a mistake. Now come on, all of you!"

"Now?" said Tharg. "We're leaving right now?"

"Yes, now. She's got a head start, and we've got to catch up with her. Follow me!"

He set off at a good pace, and the pack, disconcerted but obedient, fell in behind him in a line.

He pushed them hard over the next days, waking them before dawn and travelling until well after dark. It was both difficult and dangerous crossing the mountains, and several times Ragmarr marvelled that Kalani had not turned back. Also, though he would never have admitted it, he felt a grudging respect for Rishala, who must have followed a similar route, alone and pregnant.

When they descended into the burnt ruins of the forest on the other side, they found all trace of Kalani's trail obliterated. All but Ragmarr feared that she had been caught in the blaze, and killed. He refused even to consider the possibility, and pressed on with relentless determination, sure that, at the very least, he was going in the right direction. And when they came to the edge of the scorched zone, they came upon a single paw-print in the ash, not yet destroyed by wind or rain – Kalani's print.

On the grassland beyond, they picked up her trail once more, joined now by that of Kona and his companions, and several other wolves.

"These others must be those wolves who whispered all the time," said Luri, looking at Tharg, the only one of them to have heard Kona's tale for himself, for confirmation.

"It's not important who they are," was Ragmarr's impatient response. "The only important thing is that Kalani is with them."

The trail led them to a river, which they remembered hearing about, and they swam across as soon as they established that that was what their quarry had done. Many days later, on the far side of a forest, they reached a point where Kalani, Kona and his companions had split from the other wolves. All the time they had been travelling, the trail had been growing steadily fresher, letting them know they were catching up, and here it was barely a day old.

"We're close," said Ragmarr, with grim satisfaction. "Tomorrow, we will find them."

28
The Coming of Ragmarr

Kona woke at the insistent nudge of a muzzle against his left shoulder, and opened his eyes to see Jareth's anxious face peering down at him. He yawned, stretched, got up and looked about him. The night sky had just given way to pale, pre-dawn light. They usually rose with the sun, and he wondered why Jareth had woken him early.

"What is it, Jareth?" he said. "Is something wrong?"

"It might be," said Jareth nervously. "There's five wolves heading towards us, and not from the direction of Grassy Hollow. I happened to wake up, and saw them coming, and thought I'd better tell you. Look."

Kona looked where she indicated. The wolves, who were making directly for them, were approaching over the ground they had covered the previous day. There did not seem to be any immediate cause for alarm, since they were still some distance off, but he told Jareth to wake the others, just in case. He continued to watch the wolves as Jareth did as he said. Something about them bothered him – there was something that struck him as odd, though he could not decide what it was. Also, though they were too far away for their individual features to be distinguished, and they were downwind so he could not detect their scent, there seemed to be something familiar about one of them, the one in the lead.

No sooner had the thought crossed his mind than Kona realized what it was that had been bothering him – although as yet there had been no snow, they were travelling in single file. They must be from the cold land! At the same moment, he heard Kalani cry out as she caught sight of them.

"It's Ragmarr!" she cried. "It's Ragmarr and the pack!"

"How can you be so sure, at this distance?" Baru wanted to know.

"Oh, Baru, do you think I wouldn't recognize my own brother? We've spent our whole lives together. I'd know it was him from further off than that."

"She's right," agreed Shimook. "We'd recognize each other from that distance, wouldn't we? But what is he doing here?"

"Isn't it obvious?" said Kalani. "He's come for me! I should have known he would figure out where I'd gone, that he wouldn't allow it ... and now I've put you all in danger ..."

"It isn't your fault, Kalani," Kona soothed. "Besides, what can he do? He can't make you go back with him."

"But he'll attack you, he'll ..."

"If he wants a fight, we'll give him one," interrupted Baru. "We've fought with them before, remember."

"Why don't we just go, now, before they get here?" said Jareth. "We've got time to escape before they reach us."

"He'll just keep following us," said Kalani hopelessly. "It doesn't matter where we go, he'll follow until he catches up. He's relentless."

"We could go to Grassy Hollow," Shimook suggested. "Valzir and his wolves would be willing to help us, wouldn't they? Perhaps Ragmarr would be less inclined to make trouble with them facing him as well as us."

"It wouldn't be fair to involve them, Shimook," said Kona, "and if I know Ragmarr, a little thing like being outnumbered won't stop him making trouble. I think our only option is to confront him, to try and make him see sense. Kalani, he's your brother. What do you think?"

"I think you're right," said Kalani resignedly.

It was shortly after sunrise when the Ice Creek pack drew close enough for conflict to begin. Kona went to meet them with Kalani, who had recovered her composure somewhat, at his side, and Shimook, Baru and Jareth flanking them. Ragmarr glowered at the sight of his sister and the son of his enemy walking forward together, but it was Kalani who spoke first.

"Why have you come here, Ragmarr?" she asked him. "Why have you followed me?"

"Why have you left your pack, your home, to follow our enemy's son?" Ragmarr countered.

"Tashar is your enemy only because you make him so," replied Kalani, "and I followed his son because I love him."

"*Love* him?" spat Ragmarr. "Kalani, what are you thinking? I am your brother and your leader. You must come home!"

"No, Ragmarr. Ice Creek is no longer my home, and you are no longer my leader. Kona is my leader now, and my mate. I am going to Stony Brook with him. I'm sorry you feel this way about it, truly, but you cannot make me return to your pack against my will."

"Kalani, he's our enemy's son. I can't let you do this. If you can't see that you're making a terrible mistake, then I must make you see it. You will come home with us, or I will set the whole pack on this wolf you claim to love."

Kalani stared at him, speechless, unable to believe her own brother could treat her so cruelly. His illogical hatred of Tashar and his son was in command now, blotting out the concern for his sister that originally driven him after her and blinding him to the anguish he was causing her. Seeing her in such distress angered Kona far more than the threat to himself, but before he could speak Baru said scornfully: "Do you suppose the rest of us would just stand by and watch while Kona was attacked?"

"No," said Ragmarr with a malicious grin, "but by the time you come to his aid, he will already be badly wounded."

That stopped Baru. It was, after all, entirely possible for a group of wolves to inflict considerable damage on one in a very short space of time – even the time it took for others to attack the attackers. Then, in a calm, quiet voice that betrayed none of the tension coursing through him, Kona spoke.

"Why would you set your whole pack on me, Ragmarr?" he said coolly. "Are you afraid to face me alone?"

"Afraid?" bellowed Ragmarr, in a mixture of rage and incredulity. "Of *you*?"

"If you are not," said Kona, in the same mild tone, "then prove it. I challenge you to single combat."

There were gasps from the assembled wolves, both Kona's and Ragmarr's. Now what would Ragmarr do?

"You wish to fight me ... alone?" he said, seeming slightly confused. "Why?"

"Because I fight on one condition. You must give me your word that if I win, you will not set your pack on me or my wolves, but will allow us to leave with no further objection to Kalani joining us."

Ragmarr gave a low growl, but responded: "I have never lost a fight in my life, and I don't intend to start now, so I will agree to your terms. But you must also agree to mine. If I win, Kalani comes home with me, and you and your pack must not try to prevent it."

"I will not go!" said Kalani stubbornly.

"Oh, you'll go," hissed Ragmarr. "You'll go, when you see your precious mate beaten until he whimpers for mercy. If you really care about him, you'll stop me hurting him by saying you'll come home."

A shiver ran through Kona at these words. He was hiding his fear, and doing it well, but he could not but feel it. He had challenged a wolf who was both highly experienced in battle and more wrathful and pitiless than any he had ever seen. Yet his fear was pressed down by his rising anger at Ragmarr's attempts to use Kalani's love for him against her, and at his persecution of his father, and now himself, over what was simply a tragic accident. The concept that Tashar was responsible for the death of Brogan did not exist beyond Ragmarr's own twisted perception of the circumstances, but it was the cause of a feud that had brought them all to this.

Kona's anger surged through him in the wake of these thoughts, and he snarled at Ragmarr. As though at a signal, the combatants moved forward and the spectators fell back to give them room to manoeuvre. Ragmarr was also snarling as they began to circle each other and, perhaps inevitably, it was he who struck first, throwing himself at Kona with a savage growl.

29
The Day of Battle

Kona leapt sideways a moment too late, feeling Ragmarr's teeth along his ribs. He whirled back towards him, but he was already out of range and circling once more. Kona remembered his previous fight with Ragmarr, back in the cold land – remembered that Ragmarr had managed to wound him without being wounded himself, and that he might have suffered more than minor injuries had Tashar not come to his aid. He was going to have to be more careful.

He successfully avoided Ragmarr's next rush, but again failed to find his mark when he tried to strike. This was the beginning of a long series of such actions, each wolf hanging back, circling, watching for an opportunity, then dashing in with a snarl, only to have his rival dodge the charge and escape unscathed. The sun climbed higher into the sky as the fight progressed with neither opponent managing to damage the other, and it was nearing its zenith before another blow was struck.

Both wolves were panting now, wasting less breath on snarling at each other, and neither seemed any closer to winning. Their tactics had become so predictable that when Ragmarr lunged in from the right, Kona automatically swung left. But the move had been a feint and Ragmarr was suddenly there, tearing into Kona's left shoulder. Turning swiftly, Kona caught the remains of Ragmarr's left ear in his jaws as he withdrew, and tasted blood as the shreds of flesh tore away. The pain reminded Ragmarr vividly of the time Tashar had ripped his ears, and goaded him to greater fury. He hurled himself at Kona, crashing into him and knocking him backwards. Kona lost his balance and went sprawling. Before he could make a move to right himself, Ragmarr was on top of him, snapping viciously.

Bracing himself against the ground, Kona pulled in his hind legs, positioned them under Ragmarr, and kicked upwards, hard. His rear paws slammed into Ragmarr's stomach with enough force to lift him into the air, flinging him off his adversary. He landed heavily, severely winded. Kona charged him, hoping to tumble him as he had been tumbled, but Ragmarr, though struggling for breath, evaded him.

From then on, the battle became more intense. In vain Kona strove to sink his teeth into his rival. Try as he might he could not even get close to Ragmarr, much less injure him, for Ragmarr was drawing on the memory of every fight he had ever fought, every skill he had ever learned, and again and again he darted in, wounded Kona and was away, untouched. Soon Kona's coat was soaked with blood, and he limped from a particularly deep wound to his right shoulder. Kalani could not bear to watch, and had retreated behind the rest of Kona's companions, all of whom were frantic with worry for their adoptive brother. Ragmarr's pack looked on indifferently – to them, the outcome of the fight was a foregone conclusion. Eventually, however long it took, Ragmarr would win. He was indomitable.

The sun passed its highest point and started its descent towards the horizon, and the two wolves fought on and on. Ragmarr, though tiring, was still full of fight, unharmed except for the trivial wound to his left ear, and was clearly confident of victory. Kona, by contrast, was completely exhausted, every fibre of his being throbbing with fatigue and the pain of his wounds. Never, not even when he ran from the puma, had he been so tired, so desperately weary, for besides exertion, loss of blood was rapidly sapping his strength. Every muscle in his battered, bleeding, aching body called out to him to surrender, to submit to Ragmarr, to put an end to this punishment, but that was something his spirit – that great, valiant, unbreakable spirit that had given him the nerve to hold still before the human, kept him running before the puma, and refused to let him give up when his heart was broken – would not let him do. It drove him on unmercifully, forcing his protesting body up to and beyond the limits of its endurance.

Afternoon advanced into evening. Ragmarr was convinced that, if Kona were knocked over again, he would not be able to rise, and would have to admit defeat. He charged, as he had charged countless times before, but this time, instead of using his teeth and retreating, he collided with Kona. Just as he had hoped, Kona was thrown to the ground by the unexpected impact, and, with a bark of triumph, Ragmarr moved in. Recalling the way he had been dislodged earlier, he approached from the side, his jaws closing on his opponent's throat.

"Yield!" he commanded through his clenched teeth. Then he realized that Kona could not breathe, and was incapable of speaking. He loosened his grip slightly and said again: "Yield!"

Kona's reply came out as a muffled croak, but it was perfectly intelligible to all of them: "Never!"

With a furious growl, Ragmarr tightened his grip once more. Kona's air was shut off and he began to choke, his mouth gaping as he fought to draw breath. Dark spots, interspersed with flashes of light, swam across his vision, waves of oblivion lapping against the edge of his consciousness. If he passed out now, there would be no question that Ragmarr had won, and he thrashed about in a futile effort to escape the clutching jaws. Scenes came unbidden to his mind – hanging on to the nose of the moose while it hoisted him off the ground ... clinging to the muddy river bank as the puma fell to its death ... seeing his wolves fight Ragmarr's in the cold land ...

In his mind's eye, he saw again Shimook and Baru holding Luri and Marnov immobilised, saw again their inability to deal with his adoptive siblings' technique. And all at once, he knew what to do.

He turned his head as far as he was able towards Ragmarr, searching for something to bite. The only part of his adversary's body within reach was his right front leg. Kona seized it in his jaws, biting down until his teeth grated on bone. For a heart-beat or two he thought it was not going to work, Ragmarr was not going to let go, but then he felt the bone crack and, with a cry of pain and rage, Ragmarr released his throat and jumped backwards, trying to jerk his trapped limb free. Kona, his sides heaving, hung on and, without trying to get up, gave a violent, wrenching twist that threw Ragmarr onto his side. Only then did he scramble to his paws, keeping a firm hold on his rival and using his weight to pin him down.

"You are ... the one that ... must yield," he panted.

Ragmarr, enraged by his own helplessness, tore frenziedly at Kona, snarling madly all the while. But Kona had come too close to defeat and was not about to give up the advantage, now that he had gained it. He closed his jaws a fraction more, and Ragmarr's snarl became an agonised yelp.

"Now," said Kona, his voice becoming stronger as he recovered his breath, "will you yield, or must I break your leg?"

Kona's companions cried out exultantly, knowing Ragmarr had no choice but to yield. Even Kalani glanced back at the battle, and felt both a surge of pride for her mate and a surge of pity for her brother. Ragmarr's own pack were silent, gazing in utter astonishment at the two wolves, hardly able to comprehend what they were seeing. The impossible had happened. Their leader – their inexorable, unconquerable, indomitable leader – was beaten.

Ragmarr, too, knew it was over. The humiliation was unbearable, and he slumped back hopelessly against the ground, wishing it would open and swallow him whole. Then, with terrible, pained reluctance, as though each word hurt, he rasped: "Very well, Tashar's son. I yield."

Kona, wary of a trick, sprang back as soon as he let go of Ragmarr's leg, but he did not attempt to rise. His pack went to him, and Kona backed off to where his wolves were waiting to congratulate him. Kalani at once began licking his wounds, which were still seeping blood, and then stopped as something occurred to her. She stepped forward.

"Ragmarr," she said, "I think now you should tell the pack why it is you hate Tashar so."

The wolves of the Ice Creek pack looked at one another curiously. They knew why their leader hated Tashar – at least, they thought they did. What did Kalani know that they didn't?

"He has the territory we need, he ..."

"No, Ragmarr. The real reason."

"What? What do you ...?"

"I never dared to tell them while I was part of your pack, Ragmarr, but now that I'm not ... if you don't tell them, I will."

"He caused our father's death!" Ragmarr shouted, almost hysterically. "You know it was his fault, Kalani – why won't you accept it?"

The pack stared at him in disbelief. Was that really why he had ordered them to attack the Great Peaks wolves over and over again? Because he blamed Tashar for Brogan's death?

"Brogan was killed in a landslide, Ragmarr," said Chanku. "How could Tashar have had anything to do with it?"

"It was Tashar who always persuaded him to go into the mountains, who exposed him to the danger! He didn't even try to save him ..."

"What could he have done? Ragmarr, think about it – this is foolishness!"

"So," said Kalani evenly, "now you know why I always tried so hard to stop you attacking the Great Peaks pack."

"Yes," said Chanku, feeling ashamed. "I understand now. And from now on, I will not take part in any attack on Tashar or his pack."

"Nor I," said Tharg decisively. "I have no quarrel with Tashar himself. For the territory I thought we needed, I was willing to fight him. But not for this."

"I say the same," Luri concurred.

"And I," said Marnov.

"Are you listening to this, Ragmarr?" said Kalani to her brother. "If you want to attack Tashar's pack again, you will have to do it alone. Is it worth the risk? Is it worth losing the respect of your own pack? Your authority will not last long if you persist, I can assure you. Leave Tashar in peace. It's what Father would have wanted – he and Tashar were friends, after all."

Ragmarr looked from her to the pack and back again. They agreed with her! And she was right about one thing – they would not accept his leadership for long if he continued trying to drive Tashar out, not now that they knew his reason. He could not believe it. He, who had never before been defeated, had been bested twice in one day.

30
Homecoming

Kona had lost a considerable amount of blood, and, soon after Ragmarr and his pack departed for the cold land, he collapsed. With the help of his companions, he managed to drag himself to a nearby patch of cover, but once there he found himself almost unable to move. Kalani maintained a constant vigil by his side, tending to his wounds, whilst the others brought them food and kept watch for danger. Only after two days was he able to stand on his own, and walk around a little with assistance. Two more days passed before he felt ready to resume their journey, and then they went at an gentle pace, stopping to rest often and not travelling far each day.

It took them three days to reach Grassy Hollow, perhaps only a day's journey from the scene of the battle at an ordinary rate of travel, but there was no particular hurry. When they arrived, and voiced a Contact Song, they were answered at once and soon joined by Valzir and his wolves. The pack seemed in good health, having completely lost the lean, hungry look they had had last time the visitors were there, and had produced two cubs in the spring, now approaching the adults in size. All twelve of them stared curiously at Kona, still limping slightly and covered with half-healed wounds, and at Baru's scars, and at Kalani. But they were no less welcoming than they had been before.

"Greetings, my friends!" cried Valzir effusively. "It's so nice to see you again! But ... you've been in a battle, Kona?"

"Yes," said Kona, "just a few days ago. Could we stay here for a while, Valzir? I'll tell you everything that's happened to us once I've rested."

"Of course, of course! You're welcome to stay as long as you like, you know that. Would you like something to eat? We killed a moose this morning."

Valzir led them into the heart of his territory, showing his guests to the kill and leaving them to feed and rest. Later in the day, he and the pack returned, eager to hear Kona tell of their adventures.

"So, my friends," said Valzir, settling himself comfortably on the ground, "did you ever find the cold land beyond the mountains?"

"We did indeed," said Kona, "and I found my father, and his pack."

"I'm glad to hear it," Valzir replied, and directed a polite look at Kalani. "And who is this?"

"Someone else I found in the cold land," said Kona jocularly, nuzzling her. "This is my mate, Kalani."

"You found a mate, too? I'm so pleased for you. Will you tell us how you met?"

"Happy to," said Kona. And he did.

They spent several days with the Grassy Hollow pack, while Kona's wounds healed and he gradually regained his strength. Soon the day came when he knew he was fully recovered, and was keen to be on their way once more. Valzir and his wolves accompanied them across their territory, and bid them farewell on the other side. Kona thanked them for their hospitality, and set off at a brisk trot. Knowing they were not far now from Stony Brook gave him a renewed sense of purpose, and he was filled with anticipation at the thought of seeing his home again. His feeling communicated itself to the others, even Kalani, who was just a little nervous of meeting the pack who had raised her mate, and they made good time.

On arriving at the territory of the Beaver Lake pack, they made the decision not to announce themselves, but simply to enter Matsu's land and try to cross it without meeting him and his wolves. After his embarrassing defeat by Kona, they thought it unlikely that he would bother them a second time, and they were right. Just once they caught a glimpse of a wolf up ahead, who studied them for a moment and then, seeming to recognize them, made off hastily. They did not see her, or any of Matsu's pack, again.

As dawn was breaking a few days later, having avoided the wood where Kona had been born (none of those who had been there before had any wish to see the place again, though Kalani, once she learned of its significance, said she would have liked to pay her respects to Rishala), they stood at last on the crest of the highest of the hills surrounding Stony Brook.

Overcome with emotion, Kona gazed down, remembering how, the night he had left – how long ago it seemed! – he had stood on this very spot, looking out over the only home he had ever known, feeling as though he were leaving his whole world behind. Stony Brook looked different to him now. Smaller. It no longer seemed like a whole world, for he knew now that it was just one modest valley, carved out of a vast landscape. His journey had given him new perspective, yet one thing about the place had not changed. It was still home.

***

Annik woke, aware that she had been dreaming but unable to remember the dream. It was shortly after dawn. She slept for longer periods these days, and did not normally rise until later in the morning. She wondered what had woken her. She looked about her, but saw no sign of anything unusual. The rest of the pack lay sleeping nearby, though Garrin, closest to her, was stirring restlessly as though he, too, might wake. And then came a repeat of the sound that had wakened her – a howl, a Contact Song ringing out from somewhere up above, descending into the valley and echoing and re-echoing back and forth between the hills. A voice she had never thought she would hear again.

"Kona!" she breathed. Beside her, Garrin bolted upright, followed by the others.

"Who ... who was that?" asked Garrin in hushed tones, part of him sure he knew the answer and part of him not daring to hope.

"It was Kona," said Annik, almost dazedly. "He's come back!"

For a single heart-beat, they stood staring at each other in delighted disbelief. Then, in perfect harmony, they lifted their voices in response, Parl and Ollan adding their howls to the medley. Almost as soon as they fell silent, Kona's howl sounded again, joined this time by three other familiar, well-loved voices and one unfamiliar female howl.

Suddenly, they were up and running in the direction of the howls, filled with the desire to see their offspring again, and as they ran they saw, racing to meet them down the hillside, Kona, Shimook, Baru and Jareth. The two groups of Stony Brook wolves fell on each other in a frenzy of licking, nuzzling, tail-wagging joy, while Kalani, feeling shy and a little reluctant to intrude, hung back and watched the reunion. At length, their initial excitement abating slightly, the two groups separated again and simply stood, drinking in the sight and scent of each other.

The older pack members saw now the changes wrought in Kona by whatever he had encountered in the lands beyond Stony Brook. He no longer looked like the troubled youngster they remembered, but like a mature wolf, one who had learned much, who had suffered but

130

grown stronger for his suffering, who had stared death in the face and survived, and who had finally found what he needed to be content. They saw, too, how he carried himself with a pride and self-confidence that had not been there before – how he stood at the head of his group, and how they stood in deference to him. He had become their leader.

"Welcome home, my son," said Garrin at length. "Do you know now who you are, and where it is you belong?"

"I do," said Kona. "I am the son of Tashar and Rishala, brave wolves both, and I belong here, in Stony Brook, with the pack who raised me."

"We belong here, too," said Shimook.

"Even you, Baru?" Garrin said with a grin. "Do you belong here? I thought you wanted to see the world."

"I've seen enough of it to know that this is the best part," said Baru, returning his father's grin.

"And ... your face?" said Annik, almost afraid to ask. "Those scars ...?"

"I had a little difference of opinion with a puma," Baru quipped.

"A puma!" gasped Annik. "You have some tales to tell, it appears. But first, are you going to introduce us to your companion?"

She turned to Kalani and smiled expectantly.

"Of course," said Kona, beckoning Kalani forward. "Mother, Father ... everyone ... this is Kalani. My mate."

"Your mate!" cried Annik, almost overwhelmed with happiness for her adopted son. "Oh, Kona, that's wonderful!"

"Yes," said Kona, looking fondly at Kalani, "it is."

Garrin and Annik exchanged a glance, and some unspoken agreement seemed to pass between them. Garrin stepped forward and, with great deliberation, lowered his head and tail to Kona.

"My son," he said solemnly, "as of this moment, I pass the leadership of the Stony Brook pack to you."

Epilogue

Kona assumed his duties as leader of the Stony Brook pack with pleasure and assurance in his position. The other wolves had the greatest confidence in him and respect for his authority, and, as Garrin before him, he walked the valley with his head and tail held proudly high. Kalani was delighted with her new home, and her new pack-mates, who made her feel so welcome that she could almost believe she had known them all her life. The hunting was good, and the pack was at peace – they could scarcely have been happier. Yet happier they were soon to be.

In mid-winter came the breeding season, and as the alpha pair, Kona and Kalani mated. The whole pack rejoiced when Kalani announced she was expecting cubs. She grew large with her litter, and rather uncomfortable, and went on fewer hunts as her pregnancy progressed. The others, particularly Kona, treated her as though she was the most precious thing in the world – which, to them, she was – and willingly surrendered the choicest morsels of each kill to her.

One afternoon in early spring, sixty-three days after the mating period, she retreated into the privacy of Annik's old birthing den and did not reappear. When the rest of the pack discovered where she had gone, there was tremendous excitement, though she would allow no-one but Kona inside. Waiting outside, the others heard their leader talking softly to his mate, and presently he emerged looking at once thrilled and anxious.

"She's going to have the cubs," he said. "She doesn't want anyone there while she's giving birth, but she said she'd call us when ... when she's ready."

They stayed close by for the rest of the day, hearing an occasional moan of pain from inside the den. Kona, listening in concern, once tried to enter, but Kalani snarled at him and he backed out of the hole with a hurt, bewildered expression.

"She doesn't mean it, Kona," Annik told him soothingly, "it's just that giving birth is something females have to do alone. And don't look so worried – I'm sure she'll be fine, and the cubs, too."

That afternoon was the longest Kona had ever experienced. Every moment sitting outside the birthing den seemed like forever. Garrin, seeing his adopted son's consternation, remembered the times it had been himself sitting there. He knew exactly how Kona felt, and smiled at the memory. The end result had been more than worth the wait.

Eventually, some time after dusk, Kalani called out in a frail, tired but contented voice for Kona. With a nervous glance at the rest of the pack, Kona rose and went into the hole. He stopped suddenly as the high-pitched whimper of a newborn cub reached his ears. The sound filled him with tenderness. He hurried into the den.

Kalani lay on her side on the bare earth floor, her legs curled inwards around the four tiny, fluffy, squirming cubs that snuggled against her belly. Their eyes were tightly closed, and they cast about blindly with their miniature muzzles, pressing their noses into their mother's fur in search of milk. Kona gazed at them in wonder, his heart almost bursting with love and pride. He was overcome with the desire to nurture and protect the defenceless little creatures. Had he once been so small, so helpless? It did not seem possible.

He went to Kalani and nuzzled her. He could not speak, but no words were necessary for her to know his affection and devotion. She licked him on the cheek, and with a final look at the latest additions to his pack, he went outside to break the news.

"So, my son," said Garrin afterwards, "it has come full circle. Here your adventure started, and here it ends."

"Oh, no, Father," Kona replied, looking back towards the den where his mate and cubs lay resting, "the real adventure has only just begun."

Unable to contain it any longer, he lifted his head and let his joy howl through him unrestrained. The official Birth Song would come later – for now, he howled a Heart Song of purest happiness. Up through the valley and out into the sky his call resounded, a strong, clear note vibrant with elation. And, one by one, the other wolves took up the cry, raising their voices in a resplendent chorus as they joined their howls to the glorious, exultant melody of Kona's song.

Printed in Great Britain
by Amazon